Taxing Tallula

by
L. L. Lee

Writers Club Press
San Jose New York Lincoln Shanghai

Taxing Tallula

ISBN: 0-595-00113-0

Published by Writers Club Press, an imprint of iUniverse.com, Inc.

For information address:
iUniverse.com, Inc.
620 North 48th Street
Suite 201
Lincoln, NE 68504-3467
www.iuniverse.com

URL: http://www.writersclub.com

This is a work of fiction. All names, places and events, even if real, are used fictitiously.

For Rana who inspires me still.

Prologue

Funeral March

A constant murmur could be heard above the mournful strains of Beethoven's Funeral March that filled the crowded room. Emelda Berkley observed the solemn procession of townspeople with genuine compassion.

Miss Emmie, as she was affectionately called by everyone, greeted the people with the grave, mask-like appearance she had forced herself to acquire over the years. Although her demeanor befitted the occasion, it was incongruous with her soft, rotund features. She was by nature a spunky, fun-loving person and did not enjoy presiding over these grim affairs. But because Miss Emmie was never known to shirk her duty, she patted the sparse, old-fashioned knot on the top of her head and silently praised herself for behaving like the stoic she knew she was at heart.

Miss Emmie watched with real concern and understanding as they filed in one by one, rich and poor, black and white, young and old, her friends and her enemies, most of whom she had known for almost all of her eighty-four years. She knew she would never get used to the pain she saw on the faces of these good people as they marched slowly past the pine box, their heads lowered in submission to the cruel fates that had deprived them so terribly.

For some of the folks, Miss Emmie managed a grim little smile of pity and muttered the few expected words of condolence. But she turned away from those whose eyes suddenly swelled with tears. She just couldn't handle the crying. So, when she noticed the moisture starting to build in Tom Walters' eyes, she adjusted her gold-framed glasses and avoided the lawyer's grief by pretending to study the crude, oblong box that was displayed in the center of the large room. As if she did not know every inch of that monstrosity by now.

Miss Emmie suppressed a chuckle when she suddenly spotted old Julius Green who had built the coffin for himself nearly twenty years ago. Despite Doc Romero's assertions to the contrary, Julius had taken it into his head that he was dying of lung cancer, and being the best carpenter in town, began immediately to build the ornate eight foot box. Julius was a little over five feet tall, but the extra few feet was, he told anyone who would listen, to insure that he would have "plenty nouf room to mosey round in."

Julius was not only the best builder in Tallula; he was also the best hunter. So, he had carved deer, his favorite prey, in numerous poses and stages of flight from the mighty hunter all over the pine box. The coffin was by far the gaudiest, most beautiful piece of craftsmanship Miss Emmie had ever seen. She caught Julius' eye and acknowledged his toothless grin with a smile of appreciation for his precious contribution to the somber occasion.

Miss Emmie was careful to offer a respectful nod to old man Colarossi without making eye contact as he shuffled past the coffin. The mysterious little Sicilian was rumored to be a **compare** of Carlos Marcello during the latter's reign as head of the Louisiana Mob and was said to possess the dreaded "Mafia stare." Of course, no one could prove the old man was connected to the once powerful La Cosa Nostra, but like everyone else in town, Emmie always treated Frankie, alias The Finger, Colarossi with the utmost respect.

Miss Emmie noticed Tom Walters pretending not to notice Viola Perkins as she moved past the coffin. She smiled knowingly as she returned to the unpleasant task of greeting the new arrivals.

She had been at it for what seemed like hours, but her ordeal was far from over. From experience she knew that most would wait 'til the last moment to show up. Especially those who had trouble facing the inevitable. Like Mayor Marino. In fact, he seldom came in person. Not that he didn't care. He cared too much. Miss Emmie was willing to bet that the good mayor who normally didn't touch a drop of the hard stuff except at times like this was probably, as her dear departed Papa had been fond of saying, "as drunk as a skunk on the fourth of July."

Miss Emmie studied the reactions of those who hesitated at the coffin for a moment or two of contemplative silence. Of course, the degree of grief displayed could only be measured in terms of loss to each individual mourner. Not everyone was as deeply affected as Tom Walters. In fact, a few of the townspeople, like Cora Johnson for example, seemed almost in a festive mood.

"How's the Mayor taking it, Cora?" Miss Emmie whispered to the wiry, little housekeeper.

"He's drownin his sorrow, Lord help him, jus like he done the last time. Poor Miz Marino don't know how she's gonna sober him up before tonight. I don't know why that man don't jus trust in the Good Lord to do what's right by him. Ain't that so, Miz Emmie?" Cora practically shouted back.

"That's right, Cora," Miss Emmie answered placatingly, since everyone in town who knew and loved Cora, also understood she was just a little bit crazy and needed to be handled very gingerly.

"Is T.J. coming home tonight?" Miss Emmie knew she was, but wanted to change the subject.

"I got a big pot of gumbo jus waiting for her," Cora answered as she moved on to give Stephen Rose access to the coffin. The pleasant young doctor seemed more interested in the citizens than in peering into old Julius' pride and joy.

As Miss Emmie watched the small, ageless black woman disappear into the crowd, something struck her as being peculiar about the way the folks were behaving today. She was unaware the music had stopped, and the deadly silence caught her attention. As she distractedly reinserted the tape, Emmie realized that something was indeed different.

It bothered her that she could not figure out what had changed. Then it struck her that the atmosphere in the room seemed almost…but it can't be, she thought…yes, it is, she argued with herself. The atmosphere in the room was almost hostile. People usually accepted the inevitable with a sort of helpless resignation. Today there was something underlying the depressed mood of the crowd and it was definitely anger.

Miss Emmie had long ago become accustomed to the murmured conversations spoken in subdued tones that usually marked these occasions and no longer paid much attention to them. But her curiosity was so great at the moment she made a special effort to tune in.

She listened as L.J. La Deaux told the usual joke to Doc Romero. "Well, you know what they say about there being only two things we absolutely must do in this life? Pay taxes and die." The traditional little joke always served to break the tension in the past. Today, not one person laughed. Doc Romero didn't even crack a smile.

For the remainder of the afternoon, Miss Emmie puzzled over what was happening. She watched as the last of Tallula's citizens circled the pine box and ceremoniously dropped the big white envelope into it. When the final taxpayer left the post office, she shut off the tape player, and gently closed the lid on the coffin. She would postmark the IRS returns in the morning. Tonight she was going to the Mayor's annual April 15 party.

By, God, she thought happily, it was anger. Not once since her dear departed father, who as postmaster, started this strange, almost unpatriotic tradition to add a bit of levity to April 15-not once since Miss

Emmie had taken over as postmistress and inherited the role of hostess to these unorthodox affairs-not once had the feisty old lady ever seen the people angry.

Miss Emmie picked up her purse, readjusted the knot on the top of her head, turned to the faded and torn "Uncle Sam Wants You" poster on the wall, and in the most dignified way possible flipped him the bird. "Up yours, you old pirate. The people know what you've been up to all these years. Finally, they know."

Then, remembering she had forgotten to make her own contribution for the jerk politicians in Washington to steal, she reached into her purse, lifted the lid of Julius' masterpiece, and as if she were handling a smelly fish, she held her nose and dropped the envelope inside.

"Phew," Miss Emmie uttered as she closed the coffin.

Chapter 1
T.J.'s Little Problem

T.J. Marino was upset. Actually she was pretty near hysterical. She was in more trouble than she had ever been in all of her wholesome twenty-seven years of life. It hadn't been easy trying to live up to her name-sakes, Saints Teresa and Jude. So she decided years ago, she'd just be T.J. Not a bad person, but no saint either.

The once scenic route from New Orleans to Tallula always depressed her. Slowly, over the years, the pastoral greens and blues had been replaced by garish irritating reds and oranges of the numerous fast food places strewn like litter along the old Highway 90. T.J. was blinded by flashing neon signs and was having a lot of difficulty maneuvering her car on the treacherous two-lane highway, which even under normal circumstances demanded total concentration.

Still, her mind wandered. When was the last time she'd been home? Three months? Four? Seems like the only time she went back these days was when she was in trouble. And, man, was she in trouble. She should just go ahead and confess to Mama and Daddy and get it over with. Daddy would have a shit-fit. At first. Then he would support her 100 percent. As always. And Mama. Mama would cry, tell her she loved her and missed her and then would beg her to come home and live where she would be safe and secure.

T.J. knew without a doubt that both her parents would kill for her if she asked. They worried constantly about her living alone in the French Quarter in the big and sinful crime-ridden city. They were just looking for an excuse for her to come rushing back to their loving, but suffocating Italian nest.

T.J. knew she should have begged for their help months ago. But she couldn't. She was much too proud. And, very, very embarrassed. Plus, she'd been free from the clutches of Tallula with its small-town warmth and narrowness for too long. She might feel safer, but she could never be independent if she moved back home.

The whole mess started about four months ago when T.J. lost the $3,000 she had borrowed from her parents to pay her income tax. She had failed to ask Margaret, the accountant at the law firm to take extra withholding taxes from her bonus last year, and ended up owing additional taxes. She should have taken Josie Bradlye's advice and bought that shotgun house in the Garden District.

But she loved her small, rented apartment above the bakery on Conti Street in the French Quarter and didn't want to give it up. The Quarter wasn't just for tourists. Living there made her happy. She and her good friend, Lawanna, spent most of their weekends roaming its narrow streets, peering in the windows of antique shops and boutiques along with the throngs of out-of-towners.

The tourists were part of the scenery to T.J. Just another French Quarter character. She loved nothing more than to get up early on Sunday morning, jog across to Chartres, then to the St. Louis Cathedral for eight o'clock mass. Then she would walk through Jackson Square to the Cafe Du Mond for a quick cup of coffee and beignets. Sitting under the green canopy, she usually scanned the Times-Picayune and watched the waiters in their boat-shaped paper hats bustling about.

She sometimes made a quick trip to the Central Grocery for Italian fig cookies for Mama, especially if she had planned a trip to Tallula.

Yes, T.J. loved living in the Quarter. But buying a home would have given her a better tax break.

Actually, the trouble started before losing her parents' donation for her tax bill. T.J. hadn't told her parents what she had done with that nice, $12,000 bonus and, thank God, for some reason, they hadn't asked. Because how she spent that money was part of the problem. Her parents would die if they knew she lost it all at the craps table at one of New Orleans' riverboat casinos. And later, by actually trying to win back some of what she had gambled away, she had returned to that same enticing gambling boat and also lost the tax money they had loaned her.

And she also couldn't tell them that after she'd gambled their money away, she went to this guy that a client of one of the firm's law partners recommended and borrowed another $3,000 from him. She never should have tried to double that money at one of the casinos in Gulfport. But she had. And tragically lost his loan, too. Over $20,000. Poof. Gone. Like magic. Casino-style.

Angelo Deluca had seemed like a nice enough guy. Actually kind of cute with his big, droopy hound-dog eyes. She had arranged to meet him at Felix's restaurant in the Quarter and literally ran into him as she rounded the corner of Iberville and Bourbon. After gushing her apologies, T.J. raced past the oyster bar to Mr. Deluca's "office," a booth under the clock in the back of the restaurant.

Angelo, making an exaggerated production of rubbing his arm, injured in the collision, motioned for her to be seated, then plopped down across from her. They discussed arrangements for repayment of the loan over raw oysters on the half-shell.

"You want more?" Angelo asked, not able to take his eyes off T.J. for even a second.

"Money?"

"Tabasco."

"No thanks, Mr.Deluca. Now about the loan…"

"You're not bad looking, you know. You can call me Angelo."

"If I were ugly, I'd have to call you Mister Deluca?"

"Actually, if you were ugly, I wouldn't be lending you the three G's at such a great rate."

"Thirty percent isn't exactly doing me any major favors."

"Then go down to the Hibernia. I'm just trying to be helpful here," Angelo countered with the slightest hint of a grin so sexy it caused T.J. to catch her breath.

But when she looked into his dark, hypnotic eyes, the intensity caused her to glance quickly away.

"Look, I'm sorry. I appreciate your help and I'll pay you back a little every month. OK?"

"Sure, do you know the story of the ersters and the walrus?" Angelo asked as he let one of the plump Louisiana delicacies slide slowly down his throat.

"You mean the Walrus and the Carpenter," T.J. corrected, noticing how that little dribble of hot sauce at the corner of his full gorgeous lips really turned her on.

"Yeah, I love that poem," he laughed, thinking the beautiful young woman sitting across the booth from him wasn't at all what he had expected.

"Where do you want me to send the money?" T.J. asked, wondering what the Lewis Carroll poem about innocent little oysters being gobbled up without a prayer had to do with anything.

"Why don't I just pick it up. You know. We just go grab a bite to eat. Some place nice. Like Antoine's and you could pay up. How about I call you?"

Before she had time to protest, Angelo received a call on his cellular. He handed her a big yellow envelope, yelled to the waiter he'd catch him later and left without even saying goodbye.

At first, Angelo Deluca hadn't seemed to be in any particular hurry to get his money back, but he was charging exorbitant interest as well as a late fee. That should have told T.J. something. For a smart young lawyer, she didn't always do smart things. Of course, she had been desperate at the time. And, she didn't even want to think about where that money came from because she was just a little intrigued and very much attracted to Mr.Deluca.

No, not only could she never tell her parents that she had lost their $3,000, she certainly couldn't tell them about borrowing another $3,000 from an attractive stranger who she suspected was called Angel the Axe or Angelo the Ape or worse.

Better to check herself into the DePaul Psychiatric Hospital on Monday as scheduled. And, there was no way in hell her parents were going to know about her planned visit to the gamblers' recovery program at the local loony bin either. Or that she was going in under an alias to hide from Angelo who seemed to be showing up wherever she was lately since she hadn't returned his calls. She knew psychiatric hospitals stuck strictly to confidentiality laws and would not reveal her presence to anyone.

And her parents would never know she was being admitted with a diagnosis of depression with suicidal thoughts because her insurance company didn't pay for gambling addiction. Not that she wasn't depressed. But she definitely was not going to kill herself. Not yet, anyway. First she had to get through this weekend without her parents finding out what was going on and that was not going to be easy. Especially since she needed to borrow another $3,000 from them to cover the rubber check she had just sent to IRS today.

Bright headlights approaching in her lane quickly brought T.J. out of her disturbing reverie. "Damn, son of a bitch," she muttered as she leaned on the car's horn causing the errant driver to swerve back into his own lane just in time to avoid a collision. T.J., who never cursed when she was around others, often thought in profanities. Sometimes the expletives that spewed from the lips of the once prudish little Catholic girl surprised even herself. Tonight, as usual, T.J.'s foul-mouthed utterances helped her to relax somewhat, to put aside her distress, if only for the moment.

T.J. had difficulty analyzing the feelings of doom and anger that consumed her at times. She knew her anxiety about life was pretty much generalized. All she had to do these days was turn on the five o'clock news or pick up a newspaper and she teemed with utter disdain for the whole human race.

She worried that in the very near future, New Orleans and maybe the whole country would be taken over by street gangs. The City, her dad was fond of telling her, was not nearly as safe as when the reputed mobster, Carlos Marcello, ran things. Anyway, T.J. was afraid that someone would break into her apartment and murder her in her sleep. Or, even worse she wondered, what if she couldn't even afford an apartment for someone to break into and murder her in?

What if she had to live on the street like so many poor souls did these days? What if, in the end, we all become street people? T.J.'s overactive imagination sometimes had her living in a shack where the gas would be turned off because she couldn't afford to pay her bills. She would envision herself covered by five or six of the polyester afghans Grandma Connie had made for her over the years as she slowly froze to death. She imagined herself developing pneumonia, then dying in the emergency room because the doctors refused to treat her because she didn't have medical insurance.

T.J. knew her fears were irrational, that like many young people in their twenties and thirties, she was a product of a world gone gah-gah. "We live in a dangerous world," T.J. told Lawanna all the time. And she really believed that. She knew she wasn't really going to freeze to death. Nor, was she going to die because she couldn't obtain medical treatment. She was one of the lucky ones. She made $60,000 a year as the newest associate of Bradlye, Smith, Alexander, and hopefully someday, Marino. Becoming a partner in New Orleans' first and only all female law firm was her dream.

Instead of focusing on horrors that could never happen to her, T.J. needed to face the ones that were real. After all, she not only had a great looking little Mafia goon on her trail, but she knew he would soon be in the company of one of those IRS creeps once they found out that her check, clipped so neatly to extended form 4868, was worthless.

What kind of people thought up this freaking tax system? T.J. wondered. Probably a bunch of decrepit old men with nothing better to do with their time than to see how many loyal citizens they could screw. Men! T.J. didn't really hate men. She just didn't believe they were all they cracked up to be.

T.J. had a sensual beauty that she took for granted. She always felt being smart was what really mattered so did little to enhance her looks. Still, men, and women, too, for that matter, were always falling in love with her. She spent a lot of time saying, "I'm really flattered, but…"

Which reminded her. Mama was getting worried that she was almost thirty" and still not married. In fact, Mama was trying to fix her up again. With Tom Walter's new law partner. What did Mama say? "Eligible, thirty-three years old, handsome and best of all, Italian." Yuk. Just what she needed right now. She wasn't looking forward to meeting him this weekend.

Besides that, she probably had one Sicilian Mama's boy chasing her already. T.J. stared almost expectantly in the rear-view mirror. Could Angelo be following her? No way, she thought, a little disappointed.

T.J. glanced briefly at the lighted dashboard of her trusty Honda Accord. Another example of old Josie Bradlye's advice being ignored. "Invest in a luxury car, Theresa. It just won't do to have an associate of this firm driving, if you'll excuse the expression, a piece of junk." The Honda was a gift from her parents when she graduated from Loyola and she loved it. But, if she had financed a car a few years ago, she would have had both the credit rating and collateral to go to the Hibernia Bank as Mr. Macho had so sarcastically suggested. The clock on T.J.'s beloved piece of junk showed 9 p.m. The party started at 8 p.m. and she was still fifteen or so minutes away from Tallula.

T.J. should never have stopped at Harrah's Casino before Leaving New Orleans. But oh how she loved to gamble. Her last chance before entering the addiction program at DePaul on Monday.

She glanced in the rear-view mirror again, but couldn't tell if any of the several cars behind her belonged to the dangerously luscious Mr. Deluca. She hadn't seen him at the casino. But as usual the slots, to which she limited herself these days, had held her attention totally. Like everyone else, she was mesmerized by the one-armed bandits.

In fact, when a lady seated at a machine next to T.J. hit a $1500 jackpot, another woman who was just watching, got so excited she fainted. It didn't surprise T.J. that in the middle of loud clanging from the winning machine and rushing security guards, all eyes were on the woman gathering her coins in the large plastic cups. People actually stepped over the passed-out lady with drinks in their hands as they tried to get a better look at the big winner. Thank God, the woman on the floor came to quickly. T.J. smiled, remembering the scene. "God, I adore gambling," she said aloud.

T.J.'s thoughts were a jumble as she sped toward her little safe piece of earth. She thought of all the money her parents had spent on Loyola Law School. Of how proud they were that she had graduated at the top of her class. She wondered if, even without Mr. Carlos Marcello, the Mafia was still alive and well in New Orleans and did they still break your arms or legs or whatever if you crossed them. She thought about her dear friend, Steve, and how glad she would be to see him at the party tonight. She wondered if, after being in DePaul for a couple of weeks, and they found out she was really crazy after all, would they ever let her out? She marveled that a human being could get herself into such big shit and still be having fantasies about what it might be like to go to bed with a sexy wiseguy who looked like he hadn't washed his hair in weeks.

Or to go to bed with anybody for that matter. T.J. was probably the only twenty-seven-year-old almost virgin left in New Orleans. Not that she had any moral hang-ups about having sex before marriage. She was pretty much a horny, reluctant virgin. On the few occasions she had tried, something strange always happened.

Like the first time. When she and Steve decided to "do it." T.J. and her soul mate, Doctor Stephen Rose, had shared everything since they were in the first grade together at Our Lady of Lourdes in neighboring Center City. Since they were in their teens, Steve had often joked about giving T.J. the advantage of his own "sexual expertise" once she was ready.

One night when he was in pre-med at Tulane and she was in her first year of undergrad school at Loyola, she decided to take him up on his offer. They had eaten at the Camellia Grill and were finishing off a bottle of Chablis at his apartment on Calhoun Street. At the height of their booze-induced passion, Steve started to undress T.J., but hadn't gotten very far when she started giggling. She didn't know if it was because of the wine or because she was so nervous, but suddenly, all she could see was Sister Sophie with her sweet, pure, angelic smile.

"Do you see her?" T.J. could barely speak she was laughing so hard.

"Oh, my God, T.J. Don't tell me she's here?" Steve and T.J. often knew what the other was thinking without a word being spoken. Steve joined in the laughter as they reminisced about the innocent little nun who taught them sex education—of sorts. She must have been more effective in her red-faced chore than they had believed because here she was. T.J. and Steve laughed until they were exhausted, and in the end, they both agreed that they didn't want to ruin their precious friendship by having a physical relationship. T.J. kept looking for that someone who was worthy enough to help her lose her virginity.

And Steve never failed to greet T.J. with the words, "So, seen Sister lately?" She always answered, "No, have you?" Many times his answer was yes. Too many times in T.J.'s opinion.

T.J. and Steve shared every detail of their love lives or lack of it in T.J.'s case. Lately, however, they only saw each other a couple of times a month. After doing his internship in New Orleans, Steve chose to return to Tallula and rural St. Mary Parish to practice medicine with his old friend and mentor, Doc Romero. He had always wanted to be a family doctor and was thriving in the small town of his youth. God, I miss him, T.J. thought as she sped toward home. He'd better be at the party.

One of the small town radio stations was playing old songs from the fifties and sixties. She turned the sound up when she heard "Won't you let me take you on a sea cruise." New Orleans' own, Frankie Ford. Mama bragged about being his good friend when they were kids, and his family lived next door to hers for a few years. She had this faded picture of him in a white suit when he was about seven or eight years old. Mama had brought T.J. to his club in the French Quarter once and sure enough, the singer had greeted Diana warmly. Still, T.J. doubted he knew who the hell Mama was.

"Ooee, ooee, Baby," T.J. sang along in a pitiful off-key wail.

Chapter 2

The Party

Fair Oaks, built in 1820 and once one of Louisiana's finest sugarcane plantations, glowed magnificently in the cool, spring evening. Tom and Emelda Walters had been guests at the mansion too many times to pay much attention to the impressive white-columned structure, nestled comfortably as it was on twenty oak-draped acres a short distance from the Atchafalaya River.

"Try not to make a fool of yourself again," Emelda warned her already half-tipsy husband as their burgundy Mercedes approached the huge azalea-lined brick drive that circled the front of the three story home. Tom squinted at his obese, very overdressed wife, eyed her short, sleeveless, baby-pink sequined evening dress with disgust. Filled with self pity, he merely sighed deeply. Emelda ignored her husband's silent disapproval and chose instead to vent her chronic, displaced anger elsewhere.

"Well, one thing's for sure," she muttered, unabashedly adjusting the bra strap hanging down her flabby arm as she stepped haughtily from their luxury car, "the Marinos weren't hurt too badly this year if they can afford to have this place lit up like a damn Christmas tree."

Emelda's nasty smile was immediately transformed into one of exaggerated warmth and friendliness.

"Tony," she drooled effusively when the handsome, but slightly flushed Mayor opened the heavy oak door to greet the new arrivals. "I'm sorry we're late, but Tom here had a very important call to take just as we were leaving. The Governor himself…"

"Come along, Emelda. I'm sure Tony wants to get back to his other guests," Tom suggested giving her a little push. Surprised at this uncharacteristic gesture, Emelda gave him a dirty look. Tom brushed the two or three strands of fine hair across the top of his shiny head and pretended not to notice.

The very wobbly Mayor Marino led Tom and Emelda down the massive chandeliered hall to the huge ballroom pretentiously called the Rose Room. The Marinos had had the room redecorated in greens and blues fifteen years earlier when they purchased the then crumbling old mansion and began its restoration. The original name stuck however, and only newcomers to the plantation home thought it unusual.

The room was packed with townspeople, some who had obviously begun their somber celebration several hours before the party began. Tom caught Viola Perkins' signal to meet in Tony's library as soon as he entered the room. Viola, Tallula's only librarian was chatting with Sheriff Washington and his wife, Millie, and she hoped they had not noticed the L she formed with her left hand to let Tom know where they could be alone. Not only did the Washingtons both notice, but so did practically everyone else in the room with the exception of Emelda who was loudly kissing her hostess, Diana Marino, on both cheeks, European style. They knew that within minutes, Tom would head for the plush library across the hall and that very shortly after, Viola would follow.

The affair between the unlikely lovers had been going on for at least twelve years. Everyone in town knew about the liaison, but most hated Emelda and her bossy, pretentious ways so much, they actually condoned the illicit relationship.

Anyway, Lena LaDeau had spied the wimpy attorney and the drab but well-endowed librarian kissing passionately in the periodical room of the small parish library years ago. Lena was happy to provide the bored townspeople with something to talk about besides the very mysterious comings and goings around old man Colarossi's place.

Tom and Viola believed their little secret to be well-guarded. Folks in town couldn't figure out what the star-crossed lovers saw in each other, but they all agreed that the two were still deeply in love. Lena, who became the authority on the affair, was fond of telling everyone that Tom would never leave Emelda. Emelda's daddy had been "big in oil" and that fancy car was bought with her inheritance and not Tom's dwindling law practice.

A few people sneaked out of the room behind Tom and followed him as he eagerly headed for his rendezvous with Viola. The people of Tallula never tired of the affair.

Cora Johnson, decked out in a spotless white uniform, was passing around a tray of mushrooms stuffed with crabmeat while humming "Nearer My God to Thee." She got especially loud when she approached the bar area. Cora absolutely refused to serve liquor. She considered cigarettes and alcohol to be "the devil's tools" and "instruments of evil." Cora was not happy. She smirked when she saw Father Hebert take a puff from Steve Morella's cigarette. Cora didn't trust that Catholics knew the way to heaven like the Baptists did. She always spoke of the cheerful little man of God as "that priest." She took a perverse glee in his inability to give up cigarettes although he was trying for about the hundredth time.

She was also perturbed at Mayor Marino's rapidly advancing state of inebriation. People were used to Cora's ways and just ignored her mumblings and grumblings as she passed through the crowd.

Diana Marino was also not too happy at the moment. She was holding a couple of ice cubes to her forehead trying to ward off another in a series of major hot flashes. Diana, like her husband, was a gregarious third-generation Italian American who under normal circumstances loved people and parties. But for the past couple of years she had been in the throes of menopause and at the moment she felt like stripping off her new little silk number and jumping in the pool stark naked. Now that would take everyone's attention away from the library for a bit.

Diana looked around the room, surprised at the crowd that had shown up for this year's April 15 party, remembering how it had gotten started. Exactly five years ago, after paying hefty taxes, Tony, Tom and L.J. LaDeau, owner of the Tallula Bank tried to drown their sorrows and nearly drowned themselves in the Mayor's olympic-sized pool. Emelda and Lena came by to take their sloshed husbands home and ended up staying for a late snack.

Every year another batch of people was invited until the Marinos realized if Tony wanted to get re-elected every year, they'd better make it an open-house and invite all the citizens of Tallula. So, they'd hired a caterer from Franklin and opened their doors to their neighbors. It was always a big success and usually a lot of fun.

Diana, whose moods these days went from blissful happiness to raging anger, was perturbed when she noticed that Tony was showing the effects of too-many-to-count glasses of scotch he'd been consuming most of the day. With one muscular arm draped across Father Hebert's skinny shoulder for support, he was telling husky Lou Ella Turner, Tallula High's principal that she would look really nice if she wore women's clothes for a change. Lou Ella told him to go to hell cause she was going to wear what she damn well felt like wearing and no drunken son of a bitch was going to tell her any different. Diana approached the group with a pained, plastered smile, put her arm around her husband's neck and squeezed tightly. With the smile still in place, she whispered ferociously in his ear, "Enough, already."

*   *   *

At about 10 p.m., T.J. let herself in with the key still hanging on a personally engraved key chain she'd had since her teen years. Mama had handed her the key chain nine years ago when she was about to embark on the exciting journey to Loyola in New Orleans. Mama, who had majored in literature at LSU years ago, had begun reading poetry to her since the day she was born. That's why she knew the poem Angelo mentioned that day in Felix's. Anyway, "Child of My Heart," the title of an Edwin Markham poem was etched into the gold key chain. Mama had also given her a big hug and said with tears in her eyes, "Don't you believe what they say. You can always come home again."

The crowd's noisier this year, T.J. thought as she raced unnoticed up the wide staircase to deposit her small duffel in her old bedroom. She went to the bathroom, then hurriedly ran her fingers through her long hair, mostly to get it out of her eyes. Looking in the gilded mirror over the antique washstand Mama had found in Arkansas, T.J. applied a dab of lipstick, took three very deep breaths, then replaced the worried frown with a smile. "Time to get the show on the road," she told herself as she left the bedroom to join the party.

T.J. braced herself for the expected onslaught of greetings. To her complete surprise and chagrin, not a soul seemed to notice her staged entrance into the Rose Room. T.J. looked around for her mother who was nowhere in sight. She couldn't believe the scene before her that was being enacted like one of Gertrude Stein's weirdest plays.

Her father, more drunk than she'd ever seen him, was standing on the huge maple bar. He was flanked by Father Hebert, a cigarette hanging from his lips and Lou Ella Turner. The cheerful priest and dour principal were trying to support Tony, but both were obviously in need of help themselves. The Mayor, egged on by the boisterous guests was defaming the U.S. Government, the President, Congress, "all those jackasses in Washington who think they can tell us what to do with our hard-earned money."

"What's the matter, Tony, the bastards gonna audit you agin this year?" someone jeered. Lots of laughter. Then another shout, this one from the back of the room. "Why don't you just refuse to pay your taxes next year?" "Yeah," someone else chimed in, "let's all refuse to pay our taxes next year." "We'd all go to jail," a voice boomed seriously, as if this threat to stop paying income taxes wasn't made every year at about this stage of abandon at the annual bash.

The argument continued. "They can't put the whole town in jail," someone countered to loud cheers. "You want to bet?" the boomer challenged. "Those friggin sum-da-bitches are crazy. They'd love to make an example of our small-town coon-asses."

"I ain't going to jail for no drunken heathens," Cora blurted as she offered Millie Washington a tiny crawfish pie. "Forgive me, Lord. You like these? Mine are a lot better. These here folks are crazy tonight. The devil's talking."

"Don't worry, Cora," Millie said. "We're not really going to stage a tax rebellion. Even if we did, they wouldn't put the women and children in jail, would they, honey?"

"Sure they would." Andy Washington was Tallula's only law enforcement officer. He had been elected after his daddy died who had been elected after his daddy died. No one knew how a black man had come to be elected sheriff in the tiny Southern community long before integration. Nor did the color-blind townspeople seem to care.

"Let's all make a pact," Tony shouted. "Tonight. Now, everyone. Repeat after me. 'Next year, I'm going to keep my hard earned money. After today, I'll never pay another cent in federal income tax again.'"

Dozens of slurred voices repeated the pledge, then let out a resounding cheer. The orator and his two comrades tumbled from the bar to the isolated boos of a few of the still sober guests.

T.J. found her mother in the kitchen, seated on the floor with her head stuck in the freezer side of the refrigerator.

"What are you doing, Mama, trying to ice yourself to death?"

"T.J., I'm so glad you made it safely," Diana rose to give her daughter a big hug and kiss.

"Where are The Sisters?" T.J. always referred to Diana's siblings as "The Sisters." They were all just a couple of years apart and each either entering, smack in the middle of, or just past "the change." They were Diana's support group, but T.J. was not surprised at their absence tonight.

Aunt Frances, a widow at age fifty was probably at the small casino near Baldwin, where she could be found every night since it opened. She had quite a few critics, especially her sisters, but she didn't really care. She did whatever it took to get through the days and nights without Johnny. And it took plenty.

And surely, Aunt Annie was out tailing Uncle Carlo, who had been going out every weekend for the past twenty years. It hadn't bothered Aunt Annie that her husband had other women until the onset of the middle age scourge. Now she was obsessed with catching the bastard in the act. When she did, she was fully intent in blowing him away with her 12-gage shotgun. Actually, it was his gun, and the irony of using his favorite hunting rifle appealed to Annie's menopausal sense of humor.

In the old days, Uncle Carlo always told her he was going hunting as he left to meet one of his bimbos. He didn't even bother to take along old Sam, who usually howled all night when his master was gone.

Aunt Lucie wasn't here because she hated parties to start with. She had become so phobic during menopause that she pretty much stayed home. Uncle James, the only non-Italian in the bunch was a good old soul with the patience of a saint who didn't really mind missing the festivities. He loved Aunt Lucie with a passion that had not diminished a bit over the thirty years they had been married.

"Your Daddy gets worse every year." Diana chose not to address the whereabouts of her sisters. She was upset that they were not here to help her get through the evening. "One of these days he's going to go one step too far."

"He's just having a good time," T.J. started, then saw the effect her words were having on her mother. Lately, Mama's moods were becoming scarier and scarier, so she backed off.

"Is Steve here?"

"Yes, but..."

Too late. T.J. was already headed for the patio where she knew she'd find him. Sure enough, he was seated on the old bench-swing hung between two ancient oaks where they had spend so many hours as kids and later as teenagers talking about everything and everyone. Sharing secrets, jokes, tears. The kind of rare mingling of souls that happens only once in a lifetime, if you're lucky.

T.J. took a step back when she saw Steve practically screwing a young Madonna-looking blonde on their special swing. The young woman's blouse was undone and Steve's head was buried in her ample boobs. He came up for air a few minutes later and spotted T.J. who was just standing there with her mouth open. Without the slightest bit of embarrassment, Steve grinned and greeted T.J. as she approached somewhat cautiously.

"Hey, Girl. Seen Sister lately?"

"No, but you obviously have." T.J. answered as she sized up the woman who had the audacity to make love to her best friend on her swing in her yard.

"T.J. This is Mary Jane Gautier. She's my new nurse. Just graduated from LSU. You know her grandma. Ms. Maddie. She's staying with her until she can afford a place of her own or whatever." He said the last with a secret, knowing look as he put his arm around his latest conquest who was nonchalantly rebuttoning her shirt.

"How do you do?" T.J. said rather formally, trying not to glare. She was absolutely furious. But, she didn't know why. She and Steve had no romantic interest in each other. Or so they said. Then, why was she so pissed, she wanted to punch Steve out, then slap that little tramp for looking so good in his arms? All T.J. knew is she didn't want to share Dr. Rose with anyone. Besides, she could see she wouldn't be able to unburden herself to Steve tonight. She felt like crying.

"Well, I better get back inside. I'll talk with you later," T.J. said quietly. She turned to leave without acknowledging Mary Jane. Steve touched her gently on the arm.

"Wait up," he said, "I'll walk you in." Steve asked Mary Jane if she would give them a couple of minutes, then took T.J.'s hand as he led her away.

"Let's talk in the library," Steve suggested. "I saw Mrs. Walters dragging Tom away a while ago, so I think it's safe."

They sat side by side on the large, comfortable leather sofa that was one of the few pieces of furniture in the room. Mostly the library housed books. Floor to ceiling bookcases lined the walls and were filled with everything from the Shakespeare to Stephen King.

"What's wrong?"

"I can't tell you-now."

"Why not?"

"You really don't know, do you?"

"No, and I don't want to play games with you, tonight."

"Play games! Play games! Why don't you just go back to your little toy then? You seemed to be enjoying that game a whole lot." T.J. shouted as she fled the room.

Dr. Stephen Rose smiled as he lifted his lanky, jean-clad body from the sofa. She's jealous he thought, pleased with this development. Baffled, but pleased indeed.

At 3 a.m. when the last of the guests had either straggled or been carried out, T.J. stood with her parents and Cora and viewed the damage.

"Go to bed, Cora. The caterers will clean it up," Diana said wearily.

"Shoot, Miz Marino, it's gonna take a miracle from the Good Lord to clean up the mess that was made here tonight."

T.J. looked at Cora, thinking to herself, "If you only knew, Cora. Now, I could tell you something about messes."

The soundtrack from **The Big Easy** was playing on the stereo. As if to taunt her, Aaron Neville's "Tell It Like It Is" sounded almost on cue.

That night T.J. dreamed she was in the psychiatric hospital and the lobby was filled with slot machines. Steve was her psychiatrist and he told her if she was a good girl and took her medicine, then he'd let her play. Mary Jane, clad in a starched, white uniform unbuttoned to the waist, was coming at her with a huge hypodermic as Father Hebert, with wings, hovered overhead. She woke when Angelo crouched behind a tall palm shouted, "Look out, T.J., the walrus is going to get you."

"St. Jude, help me," T.J. prayed before falling back asleep.

Chapter 3

The Morning After

At 7 a.m., Michael Zello, alias Angelo Deluca, drove by Fair Oaks. Satisfied that T.J.'s Honda was still parked on the side of the mansion where she had left it the night before, he drove back to the old Holiday Inn a few miles away.

He hated eating alone in a restaurant and thought about getting coffee and juice and going to his shabby, but clean room to map out his next move. Michael was starving though, so he slid into a corner booth and ordered a huge breakfast of eggs, bacon, grits, homemade biscuits, the works.

Growing up in New York City, the son of two Columbia University professors, Michael was raised on take-out and restaurant food. Good food. He loved to eat. And, although his parents didn't have a lot of time to cook, both came from large Italian families, so he got his share of pasta.

Grandma Lena was always telling him he was too skinny and especially loved trying to fatten him up with her hot, homemade bread served with real butter and a dab of olive oil. He never understood how Italian men got to live past thirty the way they clogged up their arteries. Maybe that daily glass of red wine really did help.

Michael swirled honey on a huge flaky biscuit, and thought about how a native New Yorker, born and bred on Riverside Drive ended up in an obscure little South Louisiana town, eating grits and liking them. Really liking them.

Being a FBI agent had always been his dream. He'd entered the Academy shortly after graduating from Dartmouth. Because of his "Italianess" and a passionate devotion to Elliot Ness and all he stood for, he was happily assigned almost immediately as an undercover agent in the fight against organized crime. He played a very minor role in the demise of several crime families in the Northeast before being transferred to the New Orleans Bureau.

Gambling was big in Louisiana. Rumor had it the popular ex-governor, a long-time friend of the Mob, was helping the Cosa Nostra keep a hold over the gaming industry, especially controlling the slots.

Michael was a part of the Naughty Games Task Force and was posing as a small-time loan shark. Actually, his only client was T.J. Marino. He was after John Conti, who had recently arrived from Hoboken, New Jersey.

Conti was a Harvard graduate. A smart bastard. Representative of the new Mafia that was supposed to be non-existent. Conti even made the Law Review. No known association with organized crime, except he was the grandson of Frankie Colarossi who had controlled the rackets in the Bayou Country for years.

But Conti was in South Louisiana for a reason and it wasn't to care for dear old Grandpa who, it was rumored, didn't need much care. Despite his age, Colarossi was still one of the most powerful and feared men in Louisiana, yet the FBI suspected Conti was heading operations. The Marcellos were said to be pretty obsolete, that Family having lost much of its muscle in recent years. But a few years back, one Marcello relative and several New York mobsters had been arrested in a video poker case, and the FBI knew they'd only begun to see infiltration of the fading Louisiana group.

Michael knew about T.J.'s gambling problem. He counted on her not being able to repay the loan. She would be needing a favor from him very soon. Michael intended to use her to gather information on Mr. Conti. He hadn't expected to be so attracted to her, though. That could complicate things.

The plan was simple enough. Except, T.J. hadn't returned his calls. He needed to make contact with her this weekend, but it wasn't going to be simple. He had to figure a way to be alone with her, so he could talk her into finding a way to meet John Conti while she was still in Tallula.

Michael accepted another cup of coffee from the elderly waitress. He was thinking how easy it was to work undercover as a Mafiosa. He was of Sicilian heritage on both sides of the family. An Italian who looked Italian, and even spoke two or three words in Italian. He was comfortable in his role. Besides, he knew the Mafia had very strong feelings against killing cops. They might bruise him somewhat, if they found out what he was up to. But they weren't going to. Find out, that is. Michael was good at what he did and he knew it.

First things first though. Find a way to get to T.J.

*   *   *

Cora placed the frosty pitcher of orange juice on the opaque glass patio table, and thinking about the party the night before, chuckled to herself. "God," she mumbled to the sky, there's gonna be some sorry feeling people in this town today. Praise the Lord."

"Morning, Cora," T.J. said glumly, then took three deep breaths, hoping the fresh, country air would have its usual cheering effect on her. Despite her mood, the various shades of pinks and purples of the azalea hedge that surrounded the patio, and the sweet, delicious aroma from the huge magnolia tree made the young nature-loving attorney feel better.

"Good morning yoself," Cora actually smiled. T.J. was one of the few human beings she cared for. T.J. could do no wrong as far she was concerned.

"Who's joining us for brunch?" T.J. asked, noticing the table was set for five.

"That no good for nothin fool with the wife who thinks her shit don't stink, who's sneakin around with that prissy liberian, that's who. And his stuck-up new partner, that's who else."

"Sorry I asked," T.J. thought as Cora rushed back into the house to finish preparing the meal, nearly knocking the mayor over in the process.

"Well, well, if it isn't His Honor Hisself," Cora snickered. She could care less that the poor man was holding his head. She nonchalantly shoved him out of her way as she entered the house.

"She mad at me or something?" Tony asked innocently, giving T.J. an affectionate peck on the cheek. "I feel awful this morning."

"Hi, Daddy. Don't let Cora know you're feeling like the Mayor from Hell cause you'll make her day. You know how she loves to see us sinners suffer."

Tony nodded in agreement, then noticing the extra place settings, laughed softly. "I wonder what's keeping our guests. I guess old Tom had a bit of trouble dragging himself out of bed this morning, or off the sofa. Mama tells me Emelda was practically carrying him out last night. Now young Conti has no excuse."

"How come Mr. Walters' new associate wasn't here last night? I really was looking forward to meeting Mama's latest prospect for a son-in-law," T.J. cooed sarcastically.

"You must be talking about John Conti," Diana said as she joined her husband and daughter on the patio.

"Mama, are you feeling better this morning?" T.J. asked as she kissed her mother warmly.

Diana, at age fifty-two, was a beautiful woman. Although she got her lovely ash brown hair from Mary Ellen's Beauty Shop, and exercised religiously to keep her trim figure, she was one of those women who aged well without the painful benefit of the plastic surgeon's knife. Besides, she saw menopause as an enemy she was determined to defeat. So, she took her hormones and calcium and vitamins. She exercised everything. Her body, her mind, her face, her rights. Lately, it seemed to those around her, the latter a bit more than was necessary.

"Not much," Diana said in response to T.J.'s concern about her well-being. I haven't slept in two years. But that's not important. What are you wearing? T.J., you could have at least put on a little make-up." Diana was ready to be a grandmother, but her only daughter was not being cooperative.

"Aren't I gorgeous enough?" T.J. teased, pulling the Saints sweatshirt over her head to reveal a skimpy bikini top. Unconcerned about Mama's plans for her and poor Mr. Conti, T.J. had come prepared to jump in the heated pool for a few laps before she ate. It would serve Mama right to do just that. Looking like a wet, shriveled rat with no lipstick ought to kill any chance of attraction on the young lawyer's part. But although T.J. was no Mary Jane Gautier in the bosom department, she had a great-looking, sleek body.

She figured she had enough problems and couldn't take the chance that she might have the opposite effect and actually turn the man on instead. Mama obviously didn't think so.

"Put the shirt back on, T.J. And take off that awful baseball cap," Diana instructed, glancing at Tony. Ordinarily, she would welcome his input in matters of their sometimes difficult daughter. But, she was still giving him the silent treatment because of his indiscretions at the party. "Jesus, Mary and Joseph," she prayed under her breath.

"Mama, Daddy, before Mr. Walters and his partner arrive, I have something I need to talk with you about. I have a really big favor to ask."

"Oh, Oh," Diana and Tony said in unison.

"I need to borrow another $3,000 dollars."

"What? Why?" In unison again.

"Are you in trouble? You're not...?" Diana asked, mortified at the thought that any future grandchild of hers might not have a father. Although Diana was a woman of the nineties and firmly believed that young women today could do a good job of raising children without husbands, she was truly afraid of what her sisters would think.

"Pregnant? Not unless it's an immaculate conception. Of course not, Mama. I, uh, have..." She looked up as the roar of a small motor boat sped past on the river. "I have a great opportunity to take a fabulous cruise next week and I'm a little short." Sea cruise? Ooee, baby, am I nuts, she told herself.

"Short? You mean it's going to cost more than $3,000? Where are you going? To Istanbul?" Tony asked.

"That's it. Right. Turkey. And Greece. I'm going to fly to Istanbul from New York. Tour the Greek Islands. Then on to Athens before flying back to the States," T.J. elaborated, recalling information from a brochure she had seen lying around the office. She was getting so hooked on her improvised plans, she almost forgot the only foreign place she would be visiting next week would be the local psycho ward.

"Next week?" Diana asked irritated that T.J. hadn't mentioned her plans sooner. "Why didn't you say something before now?"

"That's just it. I didn't know. Lawanna booked the cruise for herself. And then, her Dad got real sick. He's dying, actually."

"Dying? Of what?" Diana and Tony spoke in unison again.

"I'm not sure. A rare, deadly disease. So Lawanna tried to cancel the trip. But, they wouldn't refund her money. Since I'm between cases with lots of comp time, I offered to buy the trip from her and go in her place. That's why I need cash. I mean, Lawanna needs the money. Because of her Dad. Dying and all."

T.J. realized she was rambling. Getting in deeper with each lie. But she didn't want to give them a chance to ask questions. She felt terrible about poor Mr. Lewis. Lawanna's dad was in the best of health and T.J.

could just imagine her friend's surprise when Diana asked if her father was suffering.

"I know you loaned me the tax money and I hate..." T.J. was trying to get back to the matter of the $3000 when a somewhat subdued Cora escorted their guests to the patio.

"We'll finish this discussion later, T.J. OK?" Tony said, standing to greet the men. T.J. didn't answer. She was staring at the most beautiful creature she'd ever seen coming toward them.

    *   *   *

"My God," T.J. thought as John Conti held her hand a few seconds longer than the introductory handshake called for. Power was the word that came to mind as T.J. studied him, only pretending to listen to the rehashing of last night's party for his benefit. Not powerful. Just plain power. He seemed so totally in control. Of everything. Despite the fact that he hadn't said more than a few words since his arrival. He had a magnetic presence that caused the small group to focus on him, even Cora who was buzzing around with a pot of Community coffee.

"Well, John," her father was saying, "we did make one momentous decision last night that you ought to know about. We're not going to pay our income taxes ever again."

"We?" Conti asked, pouring maple syrup on a warm pecan waffle, his eyes not leaving T.J. for even a second.

Cora had set Conti's plate in front of him with care, but she still held Tony's suspended shakily in mid-air.

"Me, you, Cora here." Tony laughed as the busy housekeeper slapped his waffle down causing him to jump. "All of us. The whole damn town."

"We were a little tipsy last night," Tom began meekly.

"You were tipsy, Tom," the mayor interrupted. "I most certainly was not."

"Like hell," Diana grumbled, pouring syrup in her coffee. She took a sip even after she realized what she'd done, hoping no one had witnessed her latest sign of menopausal crazies. She was becoming more and more distracted. Although they pretended not to notice, everyone except T.J. did.

T.J. was trying to study John Conti without him realizing what she was doing. Which wasn't easy, since he hadn't stopped staring from the moment they were introduced. Every few seconds, her eyes would meet his, then she'd quickly look away.

T.J. had expected a thirtyish, dark haired, dark eyed Italian with the first signs of a potbelly brought on by too much pasta and wine and maternal indulgence. He was dark and thirty-something, but she doubted there was an ounce of extra flesh under his stylish Dockers and olive tee. He was tall for someone of Italian descent, or at least he gave the appearance of being tall. His eyes were not black or brown for that matter, but amber. Almost clear. His hair was dark and cut stylishly short. Despite her lack of makeup and careless attire, T.J. didn't doubt for a moment John Conti was finding her equally attractive.

As the conversation about income taxes continued, T.J. began to emerge from her dumb-struck condition and listened. The idea of a whole town refusing to pay federal income taxes intrigued her.

T.J.'s own tax woes had caused the young attorney to thoroughly research tax law. So when Diana asked how anyone could get away without paying their taxes, T.J. jumped in.

"Mama, the Sixteenth Amendment which introduced the income tax in 1913 is unconstitutional. Look, the Fourth Amendment protects all Americans from illegal searches and seizures. In other words, it guarantees citizens the right to keep the amount of their incomes a secret." T.J. didn't stop to take a breath. "And, the Fifth Amendment prohibits the government from forcing people to incriminate themselves. You know, from testifying against themselves."

T.J. glanced at John to see if she was impressing him. She saw that she had his undivided attention and continued.

"You see, the only way the 16th Amendment is legit is if you give up all your Fourth and Fifth Amendment rights. So, the protesters simply file the 1040 form, but they take the Fifth Amendment."

"And they get away with it?" Diana asked amazed.

"Actually, they go to jail. I think."

Everyone at the table laughed. Except, John Conti. His vague grin revealed nothing of what he was thinking. Bothered by his lack of response, T.J. became quiet.

"But, what if all Americans refused to pay their taxes?" Diana asked suddenly serious again. "How would we run our government? Take care of the needy? The sick and elderly?"

"The same way it was run before taxes became so exorbitant," Tom Walters offered in his Sonny Bono voice. "I remember reading about one tax opponent who stopped paying taxes in the mid-seventies. Never did go to jail. Anyway, this guy said that if enough people refused to pay income tax, it would force the government to stop paying Americans not to work."

"Hum, welfare reform," Tony said almost to himself.

"I don't know what happened to this fellow," Tom continued. "But he was right about one thing. He said productivity would go up and there would be more money to spend. He was a pretty bitter man as I recall. Was looking forward to all the politicians losing their jobs when government shrank. Said not to worry. Private employment would 'soak up' those fellows in Washington. I loved this guy."

"But what about those poor people who are unable to work?" Diana asked, refusing to give up playing the people's advocate.

"Mama, for God's sake. We've got social security and Medicare and Medicaid." This from T.J. who only a few hours earlier was worried about freezing to death under Grandma Connie's afghans. "Mama, do you know anybody in this whole town who's on welfare? Look at old

Julius and Miss Emmie. They're going to work 'til the day they die. If
they ever die."

For some reason T.J.'s words, intended to uplift, had the opposite
effect. Diana and Tony, Tom, John Conti and T.J. sipped their coffee in
silence. Each, lost in his own thoughts, was unaware of the cacopho-
nous sounds coming from the several birds, numerous crickets and
cicadas that happily inhabited the wooded estate grounds.

Diana imagined herself with Cora in their immaculate stainless steel
kitchen. Cora was icing a huge, lopsided chocolate cake that Diana kept
insisting was not nearly large enough to hide the weapon. Then while
Cora prayed for forgiveness, Diana sharpened the 12" metal file that
was to be hidden in the cake before taking it to federal prison where
Tony was residing with all the other adult males of Tallula who had
refused to pay their taxes.

Prison, however, was the furthest thing from Tony's mind at the
moment. He saw himself being interviewed by Connie Chung who had
come back to work full time just to cover the story of the small, rural
South Louisiana town that defied the government of the United States
of America. Connie would be there when he was elected governor of
Louisiana. She would return with silver hair for his triumphant win
over Hillary Clinton for president of the United States. All this because
he had found a sure-fire method of tax reform.

Tom Walters also daydreamed of glory. He would write his best-sell-
ing autobiography from behind the walls of federal prison. When he got
out, he would be filthy rich and so famous that beautiful stars and mod-
els would crave his company. He would have to shrug them off, of
course, because Viola was the love of his life. Emelda would beg him to
stay. Promise to change her obnoxious ways, but it would be too late.

T.J. was still in the present, studying John Conti who was gazing
toward the river. He certainly was mysterious. What did she know

about him? Besides being a thirty-three-year-old eligible attorney. What else had Mama said? He was Mr. Colarossi's grandson. A Harvard graduate. What was he doing in a hick town like Tallula? Was he hiding from something? Or someone?

Everyone knew Mr. Colarossi had Mafia connections. Was John, like Michael Corleone in **The Godfather** who was sent to Sicily for protection after killing those two guys, hiding out in Tallula after killing someone? Fascinated by the prospect, T.J. turned to see what he found so interesting out on the water.

John had been watching the man in the boat for fifteen or so minutes. He was still too far out to see him clearly, but the guy was really having trouble maneuvering the narrow, bright green pirogue. In fact, the jerk seemed to be going round and round in circles. Although there was a fishing pole in the boat, and he appeared to be wearing one of those fishing caps with a bunch of fancy lures stuck around it, John knew he was no fisherman. Any fool could see he'd never handled a boat before. Especially a tricky Cajun one. John had spent several summers as a boy fishing with his grandpa on this river. He knew the man didn't belong on the river. Who was he? One thing for sure. He was obviously spying on them.

No one heard Cora approach with a fresh pot of coffee. She took one look at the silent, unmoving group.

"Lordy me, the Good Lord done struck them all cuckoo," she mused aloud, slamming the pot to the table and shocking them out of their reveries.

"Does anyone know him?" John pointed as the unlikely fisherman approached the small pier, moving in circles.

"I don't. What in the hell is he doing?" Tony laughed.

"Not fishing, that's for sure. The last batch of catfish from that river sent practically the whole town to the hospital," Walters said.

"The water's polluted?" John asked.

"Polluted as hell. Sued Clean Chem up river a couple of years ago. Lost the case. Damn crooked politicians." Tom loved hating politicians, although he considered a lot of them his friends "in real life."

They watched as the fisherman stood up to wave.

"Oh, my God," T.J. gasped as the boat overturned and the newcomer started to swim to shore, dragging the pirogue behind him.

Chapter 4

T.J.'s True Love, Etc

Michael was trying hard to look natural as he pulled himself up to the small wharf and sloshed toward T.J. and her parents and friends. It wasn't easy to look nonchalant, though. One of the shiny lures had pulled through the soaked hat and felt like it was piercing his brain. He ignored the pain and smiled broadly.

Michael had seen pictures of Conti and couldn't believe his luck as he saw the target of his investigation approach with the others. He had to think fast.

"T.J.," Michael greeted her with a hug and a big, wet kiss. "I was just passing by and I thought I'd drop in to say hello."

T.J. missed his feeble attempt at humor. She was too dumbfounded by his appearance to respond. So he had followed her. But, for a lousy $3000? Her parents and the two guests were waiting expectantly for an explanation.

Cora appeared from nowhere with a huge white towel and handed it to Michael, standing at arm's length from him. She wasn't fond of strangers. This one made her nervous, rising from the murky water like a sea monster from hell, covered in algae and smiling like a fool.

"Everybody," T.J. said. "This is my, uh, friend, Angelo Deluca."

"Nice to meet you, Angelo." Tony shook his hand. "Most of T.J.'s friends are allowed to use the front door."

"Sorry about that Mr. Marino. Uh, T.J., could we go talk somewhere?" Michael asked as he greeted the others with a nod.

"Sure. Excuse us, everyone. Mama, you can close your mouth now," T.J. responded, anxious to get Angelo alone before her parents learned about their real relationship.

She led him down from the pier, past the patio and to the swing where Steve and his nurse had been "doing it" the night before. She didn't see John Conti's reaction as they walked off side by side. He was following them with his eyes, a slight frown on his face.

"Angelo, I'm gonna pay you back," T.J. whispered fiercely.

"When? You've been ignoring my calls. What am I supposed to think?"

"I'm sorry, it's just..." T.J. seldom cried, but she was fighting back tears.

"I tell you what," Michael said. Maybe you could do me a service. Wipe out the whole debt."

"A service?" T.J. repeated, remembering how in **The Godfather**, the undertaker had to patch up the bullet-ridden Sonny Corleone to repay a favor from the Don.

"What kind of service?" T.J. asked cautiously.

Michael glanced over to the patio where John Conti and his partner were talking to T.J.'s parents. Conti seemed to be ignoring the couple on the swing.

"I need you to get friendly with Mr. Conti."

"Get friendly with John Conti? Why?"

"I can't tell you. Just get him to spend some time with you." That shouldn't be too hard, Michael thought, fighting a strong urge to wrap his arms around T.J. and wipe away the single teardrop beginning to fall down her beautiful tanned cheek.

"I'm sorry," T.J. said swiping at the telltale sign that she was about to go to pieces. Then, what?"

"Just report back to me."

"Report what?"

"Anything unusual. You know, where he goes and what he does after he gets there."

"Does this have anything to do with the fact that he's Mr. Colarossi's grandson?" T.J. asked puzzled, wondering why one Mafia guy would want her to spy on another Mafia guy.

"I told you, I can't tell you," Michael answered more sharply than he intended, causing T.J. to worry about what might happen if she said no to this deal. Would she end up like that movie producer in **The Godfather** with a bloody horse's head in her bed. Was Angelo making her an offer she couldn't refuse?

"Blood," she whispered.

"What?" Michael said, leaning closer to hear her.

T.J. reached out and gently touched his face. You've got blood here. Let me get a Band-Aid for you."

"No, it's all right," Michael answered. T.J.'s touch made him want to hold her again. He really had to fight an overwhelming desire for this strange young woman.

"Look, I've got to go. Uh, will you be back in the City on Monday?"

T.J. was afraid to lie, but she was too embarrassed to admit that she was going to be at DePaul for the next couple of weeks. Her fear of Angelo was not as great as her attraction to him.

"Actually, I'm going to be on a cruise. A long cruise. Maybe I could start getting to know John after I get back."

"How long will you be gone?" Michael asked bothered by the fact that he wouldn't be seeing her for a while and perturbed that she was already on a first-name basis with Conti.

"Two weeks."

"I'm sorry."

"Sorry?" T.J. thought maybe she had told him the truth.

"I'm going to miss you."

"Why? You don't even know me."

"No, but I intend to. I plan on getting to know you very well," Michael said lightly, looking her over so thoroughly, T.J. actually blushed. He kissed her gently on the cheek, then rose to leave.

T.J. led Michael back to the group still chatting on the patio.

"Angelo's got to go," T.J. announced, hoping no one noticed her red eyes. Maybe they'll think we've had a lover's spat, she thought. Maybe we did.

"It was nice meeting ya'll," Michael said, extending his hand all around.

When he had finished saying his good-byes, Michael astonished everyone by looking deeply in T.J.'s eyes and kissing her long and passionately before strutting down the pier without a word. He untied the pirogue from the wharf where he had hastily secured it on his arrival and tried to jump into it. The narrow little boat filled with water and tipped over. He emptied it and tried again with the same results.

Tony was doubled over with laughter. His wife watched the young man with concern, praying he and her daughter were just friends. Who was she kidding? No one kissed a friend like that.

"Someone ought to run out there and tell that young man that you can't get into a durn pirogue from the middle of the thing," Tom snickered.

Cora who had joined the group in time to see the fiasco on the river kept shaking her head in disbelief.

John Conti glared. He was watching T.J.'s reaction and wondering who this guy was and what he meant to her. The tender display of affection between the two on the swing hadn't failed to get his attention. And that kiss. Even though he had just met her, John knew that T.J. was destined to be part of his life.

Meanwhile, after several failed attempts to enter the boat, Michael tied the rope around his waist and swam off, dragging the stupid thing behind him. As a prerequisite to entering Dartmouth, he'd had to prove he could swim half the width of the Connecticut River to avoid taking swimming lessons his first year. Thanks to being a somewhat reluctant member of the swim team in high school, he'd passed the test easily. So he convinced himself that although he may have looked a little ridiculous to T.J. and the others, his breaststroke must be impressing them. He just needed to find a place to get out of the dark river so he could hitch a ride back to his pickup. He kept glancing around nervously, unaware that the rapidly flowing river had never been home to the dreaded Louisiana alligator.

*   *   *

Diana carried a small, battery-operated Brookstone fan with her at all times, even in the middle of winter. She picked it up from the table on the patio as soon as she felt the familiar warmth spread from her chest to her face. Excitement, stress, heat, hot coffee, anything could bring on a flash.

T.J., still dazed by Angelo's strange visit and knee-weakening kiss reached over absently and took the fan from her mama. She aimed it at her own flushed face.

"Well, it's been interesting. To say the least," Tom said. "But we need to be going. I told Emelda, I'd go with her to the mall in Houma this afternoon."

"Just a minute, Tom," John said quietly. "I need a word with T.J. first."

John and T.J. walked through Tony's chaotic garden where roses and weeds and eggplant grew haphazardly together.

"Is there anything going on between you and Deluca?"

Although John asked pleasantly enough, the question sounded like an accusation and added to T.J.'s growing sense of paranoia.

"Going on?"

"Romantically."

"Of course not. Angelo's a friend. A good friend. He's very passionate. That's all. You know. Italian. Like you. Italian. Not passionate. I mean you may be passionate. For all I know."

T.J. couldn't stop herself. She was so nervous. Who was this guy and why was Angelo so interested in him? Interested enough to wipe out a $3,000 debt for a little information.

"Good. You want to go out with me tonight?"

"Sure. Where?"

"I thought we could check out the casino at Charenton. You like to gamble?"

"Not particularly," T.J. said her heart pounding with excitement at the thought of going to the casino.

"We could do something else."

"No, Charenton will be fine. What time?"

"I'll pick you up about 7 p.m."

"Thanks."

"Thanks?"

"I mean, see you this evening."

T.J. watched as her father led John and Tom out, then turned to Diana who was questioning her with her eyes.

"He asked me out."

"Who?"

"John Conti, who'd you think?"

"How about that wet, bleeding fisherman who just kissed you like there's no tomorrow?"

"Mama, Angelo's just a friend. Isn't this what you wanted from your match-making meal? For me and John Conti to fall hopelessly in love and begin immediately to make you and Daddy grandparents?"

"What does Angelo do?"

"Do? Oh, do. Well, uh, he's a loan sh...officer."

"Hum," Diana said, pretending to pluck petals from an imaginary daisy. "Banker, lawyer, banker, lawyer, banker, lawyer. Wear something sexy. I'm late for my golf game."

"Mama, you don't play golf," T.J. called after Diana.

"I don't?" Diana laughed, leaving her daughter to wonder if her mother, whose memory was pretty much shot lately, simply forgot she'd never played golf in her life, or if she'd really just taken up the sport. With Diana it was hard to know.

T.J. stood alone facing the river, deep in thought. Things were happening too fast. Things she couldn't control. She tried to organize it all, put everything in perspective so she wouldn't be so confused.

OK, she told herself. This is how it is. You need to leave here with $3000 to cover the rubber check to the IRS. Chances are Mama and Daddy bought that story about the cruise, so that's taken care of. And you're going into a gambler's rehab program on Monday. That's good. Angelo is going to wipe out your debt to him if you spy on John Conti. You have a date with John tonight so you'll be able to keep up your end of the deal. That's good, too. Steve is in love with someone else and you're jealous as hell. That's bad. You trembled when a sexy mobster kissed you and it wasn't from fear of having a contract put out on you. That's bad, also. And to top it off, you have a date with another Mafiosa who happens to be the best-looking man you have ever seen. That can't be good. The only thing for sure is you're going to get one last chance to challenge lady luck. That's definitely good…and bad.

*   *   *

T.J. had only been to the casino at Charenton a couple of times. Although, it was only thirty minutes or so from where her parents lived, the barn-like casino located on the 500 member Chitamacha Indian reservation was strictly small time compared to what was available to her in New Orleans and on the Mississippi Gulf Coast.

The casino was still fairly new to St. Mary Parish and served almost as a social club for the excitement-starved residents of the Bayou Country. Gamblers came from as far away as Lafayette to the west and Houma, Raceland and Thibodeaux to the east once they learned that unlike those in Lake Charles and New Orleans, the slots were very loose. Gamblers were even being bused in from Houston. Still most who gambled at Charenton knew each other and on Saturday nights, the place was packed.

T.J. saw her Aunt Frances do a double take as she and John drove up in his new BMW. T.J. waved and signaled for her favorite aunt to wait up as one attendant opened the door for her and another handed John his valet parking ticket.

"Aunt Frances, you're not leaving already?" T.J. asked giving her aunt a big hug instead of a kiss. Diana's sister tended to go real heavy on the pancake makeup, so T.J. was always careful to avoid close contact with her face.

"I've been here since lunch," Frances answered, smiling at John as he joined them in front of the casino.

"Do you know John Conti?" T.J. asked.

"No. I'm T.J.'s Aunt Frances. Diana mentioned that you're Tom Walters new law partner. I'm happy to know you," Frances said, looking him up and down without even bothering to be subtle about it.

The threesome talked briefly since T.J. was anxious to get inside where the action was and Frances told them she needed to get home and take a hundred Bayer aspirins for her loser's headache. They were all happy when the attendant brought Frances' Harley Davidson around.

She had won the bike at the casino and surprised no one by opting to accept it instead of the cash equivalent. Aunt Frances was a hilarious sight to see. Fifty plus, vermicelli skinny with bright red hair and gold hanging from everything, riding off on that wicked looking metallic motorbike. She sure does a lot of things to ease the pain of losing Uncle Johnny, T.J. thought approvingly as she and John entered the lively casino.

The casino had been enlarged since T.J.'s last visit. The dense smoke and loud noise levels remained the same. T.J. took a deep breath and smiled.

"Do you want to eat?" John asked, directing T.J. up a few steps to Lester's Steakhouse, one of the new additions.

"I'm not very hungry. Maybe just a salad." T.J. was anxious to get to the slots, but she was intrigued enough by her mysterious date to put off the lure of the one-armed bandits for a bit.

"Sure, anything you want," John said, watching a stocky middle aged man dressed in a dark Armani-looking suit with a black turtle neck tee underneath leaving the restaurant and coming their way.

"Would you excuse me for just a moment. I'll be right back," John said abruptly, leaving T.J. alone and puzzled.

TJ didn't notice John walking toward the good-looking young man at first. Until she glimpsed the two of them heading for the stairs.

"Sure, I'll just listen to the music," T.J. answered aloud to herself, referring to another addition to the Charenton casino, a loud karaoke system and an enthusiastic little singer who was belting out a rather good rendition of "Walking to New Orleans."

She watched as John whispered something to the black-clad guy, then quickly followed them as they headed towards the restrooms downstairs.

"Shit," T.J. mumbled under her breath, dying to get to the machines, but realizing that she couldn't miss this opportunity to spy on John and his Mafia friend so she'd have something to report back to Angelo. T.J. approached the men's room and tried to peek inside whenever someone came in or out. She wasn't having much luck and was trying to figure a way to get in without being noticed when she heard her name. She turned to see Steve and his nurse, hand in hand, coming her way.

"What are you doing?" the young doctor asked.

"Waiting for my date."

"Who's your date?"

"John Conti. Do you know him?"

"Yes. Well, actually I know of him. I didn't realize you knew him." Steve had heard rumors about Conti and didn't like it one bit that T.J. was involved with him.

"Well, I'm sure he'll be out soon. I'll just wait over there," T.J. said, pointing vaguely at nothing.

She realized she was still angry at Steve for falling in love with someone else and couldn't bear to see him with Mary Jane Gautier. To hell with John Conti and Angelo Deluca and their little Mob games. To hell with Steve Rose. To hell with all men, T.J. thought as she scurried toward a cheerful moneychanger and the nearest empty slot machine.

Meanwhile John Conti and Jimmy Addolina were having an animated, whispered conversation between two stalls in the men's room.

"It's over, Jimmy. I mean it. I'm going straight."

"Whatta yah mean, you gonna go straight? You think the Family's gonna let you? They'll off you first."

"Why do you think they sent me to live with Grandpa Colarossi in the first place?" They're going to kill me if I don't change."

"I don't git your drifting."

"Look. My father said he was going to make a man out of me or else. You know what that means. I'm an embarrassment to him. To my family. It's over between us. I'm sorry, Jimmy."

"Wait a dog-gone minute. I thought you was talking about going legit. You're a freakin queer. You can't just all of a sudden go straight."

"Well, I don't have a choice. I've got to try."

"Try? Try what? You was born gay. Just like me You know, Genesis."

Jimmy was proud of his recently acquired GED. He often talked in mixed-up cliches and seemed an unlikely lover for John who was strictly Ivy League. But he made John laugh. Jimmy made him happy, when not much else did.

"I didn't know they was trying to make a man out of you. I just thought you was down here cause it was getting too hot for you up there, if you know what I mean."

"Look, Jimmy. I love you. I really do. But, I think I've met someone who can help me change. She's smart and warm and very beautiful. Did you see her?"

"Yeah, I saw the little witch. But you're gonna come crawling back to me on bended hands and knees and you know what else?"

"What?"

"Nuthing."

John left the stall without saying goodbye. His place was quickly taken by old Julius, the coffin maker, who had a bad case of the runs. Julius placed his bucket of quarters on the floor so he could pull down his pants when he heard the harsh whisper coming from the adjacent stall.

"Look, I gotta hand it to yah, trying to change yoself and all, just to stay alive. But I'm not gonna let you go. I'm gonna fight for you. Do you hear me?"

Old Julius, who had been hard of hearing for years, could only make out a few of the words. What he heard coming from that mysterious, angry voice was "hand over your change if you want to stay alive." Julius didn't waste any time getting the hell away from the bathroom robber. He didn't even bother pulling up his pants as he exited the restroom hoarsely shouting for help. A few gamblers glanced up from their slots, but nobody, except Miss Emmie who had never seen a grown man's tally-whackle, looked twice at the old guy with his pants around his ankles. She just kept staring.

When John didn't respond to his last impassioned plea, Jimmy came out of his stall and searched the room for him. He even glanced under the other stalls for some reason. After washing his hands meticulously, Jimmy left the restroom with a puzzled look on his face, determined to do what he could to break up John and T.J.'s romance before it began.

John found T.J. totally absorbed in one of the dollar slot machines. He came up quietly behind her and whispered her name, practically nuzzling her neck in the process. She was concentrating on the double bars that had just showed up on the screen and swatted at him as if he were a fly buzzing around her head.

"Ouch," John said, thinking maybe it wasn't going to be so easy after all to win this woman's love.

"John. I'm sorry. You surprised me," T.J. said scooping up the coins and filling up her large plastic cup with them.

"You want to eat now?"

"In a little while. This machine's hot and I don't want to give it up yet. I'll find you as soon as it tightens up."

"OK. I'll be at the roulette table when you're ready." John was disappointed. Now that he had made the decision that T.J. was the answer to his problems, he wanted to get on with the relationship. But breaking it off with Jimmy hadn't been easy, and maybe he needed to lose himself in the magic of the casino for a bit.

After John left, T.J. continued piling up coins and was just about finished filling a second cup when she was approached once again from behind.

"Listen, Missy," an angry voice hissed in her ear. "You may have won the war, but the battle's not over yet."

"Huh?" T.J. said, turning to face the well-dressed Italian with whom John had disappeared earlier.

"You heard me. Remember it's not over 'til the flat lady sings. That's all I gotta say."

By the time T.J. had recovered enough to question the strange little man, he was gone.

"What an idiot," she said to herself as she continued to press the spin button on her lucky machine. She didn't notice the small black lady ridiculously disguised in an outdated veiled hat and huge dark sunglasses. Until she heard the loud clanging of coins and the unmistakable voice.

"Praise the Lord."

"Cora? What are you doing here?"

"The same thing you're doing here, child. Trying to hit the big one. Now, leave me alone so I can concentrate."

T.J. had already turned back to her own pursuit of the big jackpot. She was interrupted several times by old classmates, cousins, family friends who hadn't seen her in a while and wanted to say hello. She wondered vaguely where John was and thought guiltily she ought to start looking for him. She was still winning and wasn't quite ready to give up her slot machine. Once again, she was startled by someone whispering in her ear.

"Can I see you before you leave tomorrow?"

"Steve. You startled me. Why?"

"I have something important I need to tell you."

"Can't you tell me now?"

"No, I need your full attention. Please?"

"Oh, OK. I'm leaving in the afternoon. Early. Come over in the morning. After mass." T.J. still was so angry with Steve she refused to look directly at him.

Stephen, always sensitive to T.J.'s moods, kissed her gently on the forehead, winking at Cora Johnson who was listening to the exchange as she yanked the slot handle.

"I'll see you tomorrow, then," he said softly.

T.J. watched as Steve waved to the Walters and Viola Perkins seated at the same blackjack table. Tom and Viola were pretending to be strangers.

"God," T.J. thought, "if I had this many interruptions every time I gambled, I wouldn't need rehab. One last spin and I'd better go find my date." She turned back to the machine when a weird looking old farmer in overalls approached her.

"You're a pretty popular young lady."

"Thanks. Do I know you?"

"No, but I know you." And with that, he grabbed T.J. and covered her with kisses. "And, I promise you, my dear, by this time next year, you're going to be my bride."

Cora swung her huge purse at the ardent old man who disappeared into the crowd before she could kill him.

T.J. was hysterical, but Cora soon realized that she was laughing instead of crying.

"Do you know that nasty ole fellow?"

"Yeah, I know him," T.J. smiled. Angelo seemed to be everywhere. And, he was starting to grow on her. His bride, huh? Time to find John.

　　　　*　　　　　　　　　　*　　　　　　　　　　*

"I'm sorry we didn't get to spend much time with each other." T.J. said, wondering how even God could have come up with such a perfect creation as John Conti.

They were seated in his BMW parked in front of the well-lighted mansion. T.J. didn't know what to make of this mystery man with his movie star good looks. She didn't have the slightest idea of how she should go about gathering information for Angelo. She couldn't just come out and ask him if he belonged to the Mafia. Could she?

"T.J., I really want us to get to know each other better," John said, as if reading her thoughts.

"OK. You go first. Tell me all about yourself."

"What do you want to know?"

"Where were you born? What do your parents do? Do you have any brothers and sisters? Are you in the Mafia?"

"A little town in New Jersey. My dad's a businessman. An importer, but about to retire because he's been in poor health lately My Mom's a housewife. I have four older brothers. No sisters. Would it matter if I were in the Mob?"

Before T.J. had a chance to consider an answer, John reached over and kissed her. It wasn't a passionate kiss. Just a gentle brushing of his lips against hers. Questioning. Sampling. T.J. wondered briefly if maybe John had been a priest at one time and that was his big, dark secret. She didn't kiss him back because she was both surprised and confused by the gesture. She was trying to figure out how to respond when he jumped out of the car and came around to open her door for her. As they said goodnight at the door, T.J. thought he might kiss her again. Instead his lips barely touched her ear.

"I'd like to see you again. Soon. We have a lot to learn about each other if we're going to be married by this time next year." Without waiting for T.J.'s reaction, John hurried back to the BMW leaving his date more than a little dumfounded.

"Now what are the chances of two proposals in one night? Two exactly-the-same proposals? From two almost strangers?" T.J. asked herself. She was grinning like a fool as she entered the house.

The highway that ran in front of Fair Oaks, parallel to the river, was suddenly filled with early morning traffic. The romantic closeness between T.J. and John had been witnessed by a moonstruck FBI agent in a rented pickup masquerading as an old farmer. Also by a dim-witted, but kind-hearted mobster who had just been jilted. And by a very concerned doctor-friend with a sexy young nurse draping his trim body. It was also seen by Cora peeking out one shuttered window with a disapproving look on her face and Diana squinting out the other with a broad smile as visions of bridal gowns and babies danced before her.

    *   *   *

T.J. attended early mass at St. Patrick's, the picturesque tiny Catholic church where her parents had married, where she had been baptized, made her first communion and was confirmed as a teenager. She spent a few moments after mass chatting with Aunt Lucie and Uncle James since this was the first time she'd seen them in a while. She looked around for Aunt Annie who always attended this mass, usually without Uncle Carlo.

"Where's Aunt Annie? I don't see her."

"Didn't your Mama tell you," Aunt Lucie said in a hushed tone. She looked around to make sure no one was eavesdropping. "She joined some kind of space alien religion. You know, UFOs."

"UFOs." Uncle James always punctuated his wife's sentences by repeating her last words.

"I'm sure," T.J. laughed. "Aunt Annie's a saint. She would never leave the Catholic Church."

"Well, she did. And not only that. She goes around preaching this craziness to everyone. Telling us that God is from another planet. I hear she even claims to have been abducted. I run every time I see her coming. Scares me to death."

"To death," Uncle James said.

T.J. discussed Aunt Annie's desertion to her strange new religion for a while longer then realized Steve would be waiting back at the house. After saying goodbye, she ran to her Honda. She couldn't help worrying about Aunt Annie though. Wondering if it was menopause or Uncle Carlo's philandering that had sent poor Aunt Annie over the edge.

Stephen was waiting for her when she got back. They sat on the patio sipping orange juice and eating Honey Nut Cheerios over the loud protests of Cora who was pushing bacon and eggs and homemade biscuits.

"So what's so important that we had to be alone before you could tell me?"

"Why are you so pissed at me, T.J.?"

"I don't know what you're talking about."

"This is about Mary Jane, isn't it. You're jealous."

"Why would I be jealous of Super Nurse. Just because she's gorgeous and has huge boobs and you can't keep your hands off her."

Steve laughed and after a while, T.J. laughed with him. Cora brought out a pot of coffee, humming Rock of Ages, her eyes darting between the two of them, causing them to laugh even harder.

"I missed you."

"I've been here all weekend."

"Well, what about you and John Conti?"

"What about us? I mean there is no me and John Conti."

"That's not what it looked like last night."

T.J. responded with a puzzled look.

"I just happened to be passing by and saw the two of you uh, saying goodnight."

"Then, you know I didn't see Sister last night. Come on, Steve. I hardly know the man."

"You might want to keep it that way."

"Why?"

"Trust me. I've heard some things I wouldn't want you to get hurt."

"What have you heard? Tell me."

"Just stay away from him. OK?"

"You know, you're really something. Trying to tell me who I need to go out with. Even being friends for a hundred years doesn't give you the right..."

"No, but if you're going to be my wife by this time next year, then I think that gives me the right."

"Your wife?"

"My wife." And with that Stephen gathered T.J. in his arms and kissed her. Quietly at first and then with a pent up passion that even he didn't realize he felt for his best friend.

Cora, approaching quietly with a big bowl of fruit, couldn't believe what she was seeing. Three men fawning all over T.J. in one weekend. This girl needs to get married and settle down, Cora thought. "Lord, help us," she said.

Chapter 5

The Loony Bin

"What do you mean, you got three marriage proposals over the weekend?" Lawanna was stretched out on T.J.'s blue and white striped sofa. T.J. had arrived back in New Orleans early Sunday afternoon and had called her friend immediately. She was so confused and needed desperately to talk with someone.

Lawanna usually spent long hours as an intern at Charity, the state hospital with the new name that no one could remember. So T.J. was relieved to find her at home and bored. The two young women had been close since their freshmen year at Loyola and truly loved each other. T.J. had been too embarrassed at first to tell her friend how her gambling had caused her to be in such a fix.

But for the past couple of hours she had shared every gory detail of her recent ordeal and weird weekend. It was better than going to confession because Lawanna was so accepting of T.J.-no matter what. No penance at all.

"Yes, three. And you know what? I might just marry one of them."

"Which one?"

"Well, that I don't know. Yet. But Angelo is so exciting. I know he's probably in the Mafia and all and he's only vaguely familiar with the English language. But talk about sexy. I actually tremble when he touches me. Can you believe it? Me? Acting like a school girl around a greasy little loan shark."

"No, Tee," Lawanna laughed, almost choking on her diet soda as she reached for a chocolate covered cherry. Lawanna was always trying to lose weight, but despite being a doctor with a solid understanding of good nutrition, she absolutely adored chocolate. 'Chocolates be good for this li'l chocolate gal' she liked to joke.

"What about Steve? I always thought you protested a bit much about not being romantically involved with him."

"I love Steve. He's my friend. My soulmate. And I have to admit, I was pretty pissed when I saw him with that bitch with the big boobs. Lawanna, he kissed me. I mean, really kissed me for the first time ever. It felt good. Right. Quite wonderful, in fact. Do you think I'm crazy not to know my heart?"

"Of course I think you're nuts. What about **bachelor-number-three**? The lawyer your Mamma was going to fix you up with?"

"John Conti. Now talk about a mystery man. He is the best looking son-of-a-gun I have ever seen. He exudes, confidence and power, yet is very gentle. He doesn't say much. And I think Angelo thinks John's in the Mafia, too. Maybe there's some kind of Mob Family rivalry thing going on. I don't really know. All I know is I want to get to know Mr. Conti a whole lot better."

"So, what are you going to do now?"

"Go to Disneyworld."

"Huh?"

"I'm checking myself into DePaul tomorrow. I have to get this gambling under control and I need for you to do a couple of things for me."

"Sure. Anything."

"Deposit this check from my parents for me. I won't have time in the morning and if you don't, my check to IRS is gonna bounce."

"What else?"

"If anyone, especially my parents, call you for any reason, I'm on a cruise in the Greek Islands. OK?"

Lawanna just raised an eyebrow.

"Oh, one other thing. If my parents want to know how your Dad is doing, tell them he has made a miraculous recovery."

"Girl, I think you have a little more confessing to do here."

"Right."

As usual the two friends talked long into the night.

*   *   *

DePaul's original red brick building erected in the early 1830's had disappeared with Betsy, the hurricane that most residents of New Orleans still mention in hushed, reverent tones.

The Seton Building, built in 1938 was named after Elizabeth Seton, the founder of the Daughters of Charity. It was reportedly still haunted by Mother Seton herself and despite the fact that it was surrounded by modern structures, most new arrivals were scared to death. T.J. imagined all sort of horrors beyond its secret walls. That's why she left her battered duffel bag in the trunk of her car. Just in case she couldn't go through with this.

As she headed for the entrance, T.J. almost turned back, telling herself that she just had a teeny gambling problem, not an addiction after all. Somehow she managed to get directions to the admitting office and found herself knocking timidly on the first door she came to.

"You're here. Thank God." She was greeted by a tiny harried looking woman who motioned for her to come in. "You're a bit late, but don't worry. We can do the paper work later. Let's just get you to the unit. Stat!"

Before T.J. had a chance to open her mouth, she was being whisked down long, dark and very narrow corridors by this strange little woman who hadn't even bothered to introduce herself. Her guide stopped abruptly, nearly knocking T.J. off her feet. She yanked a pile of keys from her orange blazer and opened a large heavy door with several lay-ers of peeling paint. The door clanged shut behind them, causing T.J. to literally leap in the air.

"Here we are. Mary Anne is going to introduce you around and give you a brief orientation to start," she said nervously. "I'll bring your papers along shortly. Well, I don't see her, but I'm sure she's around. Just wait here. OK?" She was gone in a flash.

"OK," T.J. answered to the orange blur as she looked cautiously around, half expecting a bunch of crazy people to jump out from behind a huge battered-looking plastic ficus tree and yell "surprise." The deserted nurses station overlooked a fairly large open room with well worn sofas and game tables and a T.V. A massive hole in the wall behind one of the sofas was only half concealed by a Mardi Gras print depicting two ominous looking masks. T.J. was terrified and backed slowly toward the door when suddenly it was unlocked. About a dozen or so ancient-looking people filed in, followed by a vibrant, very obese white haired lady dressed in a sixtyish polyester pants suit.

"Hi honey. I'm Mary Anne Landry. I'm glad you made it. I'm sorry I wasn't here to welcome you. We had our little morning walk around Audubon Park. But you're just in time for group."

T.J. saw that a few of the old guys were slowly moving bile green plastic chairs to form a circle of sorts and moved quickly to help them. It took a while for everyone to be seated, so T.J. got a chance to briefly observe the other patients on the unit.

She was trying not to stare, but she was puzzled by the fact that almost everyone seemed to be at least 100 years old. She knew lots of little ole ladies gambled away their grocery money, even their whole social security checks, but this was ridiculous. These folk hardly appeared to be high rollers. Hell, most could barely move.

"OK, everyone. You know what to do. Introduce yourself. Then say why you're here. Let's start with you, Joe."

"Listen, Nurse Ratchet. If I told you once, I've told you a thousand times. My name is Mr. Joseph Brownell, III and it's nobody's business but my own why I'm in this God-forsaken place with all these old crazies."

"Who you calling crazy, you old geezer?" a black haired lady with a huge bald spot shouted. "Everybody knows you got the old timer's disease."

"Yeah, and everybody knows you like to take a little nip every now and then. And more now than then, Mizz Stanton."

"Joe, Hillary. That's enough." Mary Anne turned to T.J. "Joe, uh, Mr. Brownell and Hillary really get along fine. Hillary, you were telling us yesterday about how you slipped during Mardi Gras."

"Well, I was hosting my annual party on St. Charles during the Bacchus parade, you understand," Hillary yelled at T.J.

"Hillary comes in once a year to dry out," Mary Anne explained to the newcomer. "Billie, you're next."

"I'm Whilhemina Breaux. I've been clinically depressed since Charlie left me."

"Your husband?" T.J. asked bravely, still wondering what in the hell she was doing here with all these strange old people. They were really starting to scare her.

"Of course not, you silly girl. You think I'm nuts? I've had three husbands leave me. All are in the bosom of the Good Lord. Except maybe Larry. He tended to cheat on his income taxes. Big time. Enough, in fact, to burn in hell for all eternity." Billie made the sign of the cross before continuing. "No, dear. Husbands can be replaced. But, not Charlie. I sneaked him in from Cozumel years ago. He was my best friend. I don't know why he left me." Billie started sobbing as she talked about the loss of her pet iguana.

"Well, Bill Clinton probably stole Charlie." T.J. glanced at the huge black man who had angrily spat out the words.

"No, Louis," Mary Anne soothed, "Clinton did not take Charlie."

"Yeah, he did. Just like he's stealing my color. You can't tell me the man's not putting something in our water supply to turn us white. Look here. Look at this hand. White. Filthy white."

The giant stood and shoved his massive hand in front of T.J.'s ashen face. She scooted her chair back and raised her arm to ward off the expected blow. Between extended fingers, she peeked at Louis's big, black hand, half expecting to see it fade before her eyes.

"You want to talk about thieves? I'll tell you about thieves. Oh. By the way, I'm Frank Peronio and I'm in here because my kids think they can declare me incompetent. Ha. Me. Incompetent. Can you believe it? I'm a rich man. A very rich man. But I cut them off. Wrote a will. Gave every cent of my hard earned dollars to Dollie."

"The stripper," several group members offered in unison to T.J.s questioning look.

At the word, stripper, a quiet angelic looking woman started to unbutton her blouse. Mary Anne mouthed "no" to her and she stopped immediately.

"Yeah," Frank continued with a wide grin. "You seen her act on Bourbon Street?"

"No, I don't…"

But before a now terrified T.J. had a chance to explain she didn't frequent the strip joints in the Quarter, Frank resumed his tirade against his family.

"And now they want to steal my money to spite me. Ha. Just let them try."

T.J. tuned out the rest of Frank Perino's grievances and heard only snatches of what the next couple of patients had to say. She was trying to decide how she was going to get out of this geriatric cuckoo's nest when she noticed one comatose-looking old fellow making a move on a feisty silver haired lady. He appeared to be winking at T.J., but once he closed the one eye, he couldn't seem to get it reopened. As the old gal inched her chair away from him, he looked at her out of the corner of the unstuck eye and reached over nonchalantly to pinch her on the behind. She put both hands together as if to pray and swung fiercely, slamming into his head. His stuck eye popped open and he gave the object of his unwanted attentions a large toothless grin. Everyone but T.J. ignored the two of them. T.J. glanced around, casing out nearest exits, her heart pounding.

Someone named Barbara Cohen introduced herself to T.J., then jumped up and grabbed her hand. An already shaken T.J. almost passed out as the overweight elderly lady pumped her arm furiously for what seemed like forever. Then, dropping T.J.'s hand like it was a hot potato, she immediately pulled out a packet of those wipes that you clean baby bottoms with and used up the whole bunch wiping off T.J.'s germs.

"It's part of Barbara's program to touch people so that she'll become less and less concerned with cleanliness. She's doing really well. Isn't she, group?"

"Yeah," several group members admitted begrudgingly. Barbara smiled nervously.

"It's your turn, dear."

T.J. who was pretty much hysterical by now didn't realize that they had gone almost full circle and everyone was looking at her. Suddenly, she blurted:

"I'm T.J. Marino and I'm here because I'm a compulsive gambler and I've lied and cheated to my parents and I've borrowed money from everybody I know including this Mafia guy who says he wants to marry me. And I have to decide about him and about Steve who's a doctor and John who's also in the Mafia cause they proposed, too."

T.J. couldn't stop herself. "But first I have to get my shit together with this gambling problem."

Everyone stared at T.J. like she had just admitted she was a mass murderer. While Mary Anne seemed to be shocked into silence for the first time in a while, Mr. Brownell spoke up.

"Nurse Ratchet, I know I'm supposed to be sick in the head and all these other folk are crazy as loons, but none of us are fools. Why in the world would you people hire a young social worker with worse problems than us?"

"Everybody. Let's take a break. T.J. Honey, can we talk?"

*   *   *

T.J. and Mary Anne were standing in front of the nurses station trying to figure out how T.J. ended up in the Personnel Office rather than the Admit Office. Mary Anne was explaining that everyone, herself included, naturally assumed she was the new social worker who had been expected that very morning.

"I'll just call someone from Admit to pick you up and take you to the Addictive Disease Unit, OK?"

A badly shaken T.J. was about to tell Mary Anne that it was most certainly not okay when a shrill doorbell sounded, causing her feet to leave the ground again.

Mary Anne used a key from a set of a dozen or so hidden in the pocket of her pants. T.J. watched as she admitted a vaguely familiar looking man in a khaki uniform. T.J.'s eyes shifted to the nametag that identified him as Clarence Greene, Plant Operations. As he approached the nurses station, smiling pleasantly at Mary Anne, T.J. realized that he was Angelo. I'm saved, she thought, as she rushed into his arms was. I'm saved.

Some of the group members were shuffling around nearby in hopes of eavesdropping in on T.J.'s continuing saga. Mr. Brownell whispered loudly to Frank Peronio something to the effect that "the young nutcase probably had one of those so-called sexy addictions instead of a gambling problem." Frank Peronio agreed wholeheartedly since the "pretty li'l thing sure threw herself at that maintenance guy like she was love starved or something."

"Angelo," T.J. sobbed with relief, "I'm so happy to see you. Will you take me home, please?"

"Not now, T.J." Mary Anne soothed, thinking this young lady had more than an addiction problem. She was delusional as hell.

"Mr. Greene has work to do. And we need to get you to Admit."

"Angelo, get me out of here. Now!" T.J. screeched.

"Uh, excuse me, Miss. My name is Clarence Greene. I must just look like your friend, Angelo."

"Angelo, please. You know me. T.J. Your bride to be," she said sarcastically.

"I'm sorry, Miss, my fiancée' is on a cruise."

Michael glanced toward the dayroom, avoiding T.J.'s pitiful expression of hurt and budding anger.

"I guess that's the hole I'm suppose to fix. I'll just step over there and measure if you don't mind, Miss Landry."

Michael had no idea what T.J. was up to, but she deserved to suffer a bit longer for lying to him.

"Sugar," Mary Anne said, taking T.J. gently by the arm. Mary Anne always overdid the endearments when she felt sorry for someone. And she was concerned about this poor girl who thought she was engaged to the maintenance man.

"Sweetheart, sit down here for a minute while I call Admit."

She pulled a plastic chair up close to the station.

"Don't you touch that phone," T.J. said in her steely lawyer voice.

"Sweetheart,…"

"No. No sweetheart. I want out of here. Now."

"But T.J. honey, you really need to give us a chance. Let us evaluate you, baby. OK?"

"You're not hearing me." T.J. forgot to be scared. She was so angry at Angelo, she felt like going over there and letting him have it. But first things first.

"I was never admitted to this hospital in the first place."

"I understand, baby. But you're upset. Let me just get somebody from Admit on the phone…"

"Look, lady. I may be having a few problems right now, but if you don't let me out of here this very minute, you're going to be sorry. I'm a lawyer and I'll sue your ass for false imprisonment so fast, you'll be sorry you ever laid eyes on me. Is that clear enough?"

"Sure, baby. I mean T.J. Anything you say. I'll just unlock the door and direct you to the nearest exit."

T.J. gave Angelo a furious look, but smiled sweetly to the few group members who had gathered round to hear the confrontation. The group applauded T.J.'s boldness as she rushed out of the unit.

Michael pocketed a tape measure as he raced toward the door still being held ajar by the amazed nurse. He sped after T.J. and caught up with her as she fumbled to get her car door opened. He grabbed her by the arm, trying hard not to laugh.

"I'm sorry," he managed, barely able to keep a straight face. "What was that all about?"

"You stay away from me, you bastard. You hear me. I don't want to see you, hear you…"

Michael realized that he had fallen totally in love with this woman. He looked deeply into her eyes, now sparkling with anger. He pulled her toward him and brought his face close to hers. She jerked away from him, jumped into her car and sped off, leaving him standing there, staring after her and wondering what in the world he was going to do about his feelings for her.

Chapter 6

Sea Cruise

T.J. tried unsuccessfully to call Lawanna when she got back to her apartment. She left a message asking her friend to return her call as soon as possible, then fixed herself a cup of herbal tea to see if she could calm herself down long enough to figure out what to do.

She had ten days, two weeks actually to do something to turn her life around. She was not going back to the hospital. She did not have to be at work. She could take a trip. A cruise. Why not? Not a big, expensive Greek cruise. But a little jaunt from New Orleans to the Caribbean. The ships left weekly. Yes! A little gambling cruise to the Islands. "Now that would make me happy. That would make me forget all my troubles for a while," T.J. thought as she reached for the phone to let Lawanna's answering machine know her plans.

T.J. busied herself for the next hour or so making the travel arrangements, packing, thinking. She was still so angry at Angelo for not helping her. She wondered how he knew she was at the hospital in the first place. She realized he must have followed her. But why? T.J. really did need some time out. To figure out why her life was so screwed.

She held up a black sleeveless shift, thinking all she really needed was a couple of pair of jeans. She decided to pack the dress just in case. She took a pair of warm-ups and all of her toiletries from the duffel and switched them to the larger suitcase, thinking this was going be fun. No Angelo to make her crazy. No Steve to confuse her. No John Conti to intrigue her. No boss to harass her. No friends or aunts or parents to smother her.

She planned to go into hiding for the next week or so. She would check into the Riverside Hilton tonight and board the cruise ship in the morning. Just T.J. responsible for T.J. for a change. Yeah, this was just what she needed. And she would make damn sure Angelo Deluca wasn't following her this time.

Right, T.J. thought happily. A gambling cruise is going to be a hell of a lot more fun than a psychiatric hospital and what I need right now is fun, fun, fun. "Ooee, ooee, baby," she sang softly before calling a cab.

      *   *   *

Michael paid little attention to his driving as he sped along Highway 90 in his Tulane-green Jeep Wagoneer. He should have been in Lake Charles hours ago. He had planned to stop in Morgan City for lunch at his favorite Holiday Inn, but he drove past the small town, thinking he'd have to settle for a sandwich at the McDonalds in Lafayette before getting on the Interstate there.

The trip from New Orleans was taking forever. He found himself slowing down and speeding up in rhythm with his erratic thoughts about T.J. He should have been thinking about John Conti and what he would find in Lake Charles. Instead, T.J. kept invading his brain. He was bothered that she had lied to him about going on a cruise. How she ended up at DePaul with a bunch of old loonies, he couldn't even begin to imagine.

He had followed her this morning hoping to catch a glimpse of her as she headed out to the airport. He was confused when she started up St. Charles Avenue instead, ending up in the DePaul parking lot.

Following her into the hospital had been easy. Even getting onto the unit had been a snap. He was, after all, somewhat of a master of disguise. What wasn't so simple was trying to figure the woman out.

He had jokingly declared his love for her with the half-hearted marriage proposal, which she obviously hadn't taken seriously. In fact, he knew he didn't have a chance with her as long as she thought he was a wiseguy. Or as long as John Conti was in the picture for that matter.

John Conti. The reason for this little trip to Lake Charles. An informer reported seeing Conti hanging out at the two casino boats in Lake Charles pretty frequently in the past few months. He was said to have been in the company of a small time punk called Jimmy Addolina. The informer, a long time Mob associate and recent friend of the FBI said he'd be at the Players Island hotel next to the boats. Michael hoped he wasn't going to arrive too late as he pushed down on the accelerator.

Michael felt himself relax as he drove through the part of Louisiana known as Cajun Country. It was just April, but everything was so green. The moss-laden majestic oaks that lined the highway were huge. He's never seen anything like them growing up in the City.

As he drove through Lafayette, his stomach started growling. It was crawfish season and he loved those little buggers. If he weren't so late, he'd stop at Don's and have a couple of pounds. He realized that the drive-thru at McDonalds was going to have to do.

A local radio station was playing "Zydeco Gris Gris" and as he beat out the rhythm on the Jeep's steering wheel, thoughts of T.J. came back like a pacifier, replacing the craving for the spicy mudbug. He hadn't had time to follow her back to her apartment. He hoped she was OK. Maybe he'd call her tonight. To talk business. To hear her voice. He should be in Lake Charles by 3 p.m. Maybe he'd call her then.

*   *   *

Dr. Stephen Rose was advising Father Hebert on the use of the nicotine patch.

"Now, I know you can get these things over the counter these days. But you need to be careful. You want to avoid nicotine withdrawal, and there are side effects if you overdo it."

"Look, Stephen, I plan to be around a long time, if the Good Lord is willing. I hear every word. The patches work better than anything else I've tried. Especially that gum. It didn't get along real well with my fancy new bridgework. Look, I'll be a good boy. I'm a man of God, you know."

"Yeah, I know. I should, considering."

"Maybe it'd be better if we change the subject. I don't need to be preached to by a former hell raiser of a student, even if he is a smart-ass doctor now and my saintly, deteriorating body is in his hands. And the Good Lord's, you know."

"Yeah, I know," Steve laughed. He loved teasing the little priest about the old days when he had made the man's life miserable. Stephen's angelic looks had always belied his capacity for causing trouble and Father Hebert had spent hours trying to help the nuns at Our Lady of Lourdes manage him.

Father Hebert smiled at Stephen as the young doctor wrote out his prescription for Zocar, the only thing that kept his cholesterol level down, since his love of good food and wine was almost as great as his passion for cigarettes.

The priest held a special place in his heart for Stephen and had since that very first day when the scared little boy appeared with his widowed mama for his first day of kindergarten so many years ago.

Claire Rose had mysteriously appeared in Tallula. Rumors spread quickly around the small town. That she was from Chicago. That her husband had been killed in Vietnam. That she was really divorced. That she had never been married at all. That her secret lover and father of her child was a married man from Tallula. Why else would she chose to live in a town where she did not know one soul?

Over the years, however, most of the questions about her past faded. Claire Rose lived quietly with her son in a makeshift apartment in L.J. La Deaux's mama's rambling old home. She got a job weighing vegetables at the Winn Dixie in Morgan City, and worked her way up to manager of the produce department.

No one could figure out how she was able to afford to send Stephen to the Catholic school on her salary except that maybe her secret lover was a man of means. This rumor was fueled when Stephen entered Tulane. Everyone knew the venerable old university was one of most expensive in the South, perhaps in the whole country.

Father Hebert took the prescription from Stephen and rose to give his friend a hug when the phone in his office rang.

"Mary Jane, would you tell him I'll call him back? What? OK, put him on," Stephen waved to the priest, then pressed the line that held the caller. As he left the office, Father Hebert heard the young man hiss into the phone.

"I told you never to call me at this office. Here I am Doctor Stephen Rose. This had better be an emergency. And I don't mean a medical one."

      *   *   *

John Conti smiled patiently as he faced T.J.'s mother and aunts seated in a semicircle in the attractive, soft leather chairs in his plush office. He was advising Diana and her sisters on now to best dissolve their small corporation. The business had been established fifteen or so years earlier when their daddy, a wealthy sugarcane grower, had left them a thousand acres of land that they promptly converted into a lucrative housing subdivision.

Most of the lots had been sold years ago and there was no reason to undo the partnership at this time except the women wanted a closer look at Mr. John Conti. In fact, when Tom Walters insisted on helping them himself, Diana threatened to never speak to him again if he didn't set it up with his young associate.

So here they were. Frances, as wild-looking as ever in a short, black leather miniskirt. Lucie, fanning herself with an old magazine that featured a boa wrapped, otherwise practically nude, Dennis Rodman. Annie, hands folded as if in prayer nodding approval of the young man to the others. And Diana, deciding that the young lawyer was definitely son-in-law material.

John had spent most of the hour trying to learn as much as he could about T.J. without seeming too eager or inexperienced in his pursuit of her. The Sisters certainly were more than happy to share anything and everything that would lead to a march down the aisle for the potential lovers and in their overzealousness, kept interrupting and correcting each other. John hoped a fight wouldn't break out before he got all the particulars about the Greek cruise she was on. There was no reason in the world he couldn't fly out to the Islands and surprise her.

As he escorted The Sisters to the door and took each of their hands in his, T.J.'s Aunt Frances winked knowingly at him. She lagged behind so that she could whisper her secret to him.

"This is just between you and me. I've already picked out the perfect caterer for the wedding reception. A Mr. Streva. From Franklin. He throws a real old-fashioned Italian party."

"But, how could you…?"

"From the moment I saw you and T.J. together at the casino, I just knew you were made for each other."

"Hmm…"

"Mum's the word. I'll tell Diana as soon as the two of you announce your engagement. Just because she's the mother of the bride doesn't entitle her to all the fun."

As soon as the women left, John instructed Louanne, the mousy looking receptionist hired by Emelda Walthers, to try to locate Dr. Lawanna Lewis. "She's doing her internship at Charity Hospital in

New Orleans. Have her paged." According to Diana, T.J.'s good friend would know all the particulars about the cruise she was on.

*   *   *

John packed hurriedly. He had a two-hour drive ahead of him to the airport in New Orleans. There he would board the private plane owned by "friends" of Grandpa Colarossi that would carry him to the Islands and his rendezvous with T.J.

Earlier, when a harried-sounding Lawanna had come to the phone, he told her who he was and what he intended. T.J.'s friend had balked at first.

"She doesn't want anyone to know where she is. She really needs to be alone for a while. I'm sure you understand."

"Look, I know you're her friend and are just being protective of her, but I really need to talk with her."

"Why?"

"Because I love her."

That simple statement did the trick, because although Lawanna didn't know exactly what cruise ship T.J. was on, she did know that it had left the City on Tuesday for a seven-night excursion to the Caribbean.

John thanked the young intern quietly before having Louanne check the cruise lines in New Orleans to see which one left on Tuesday.

*   *   *

T.J. had been on the ship for three days and she had not gone near the casino one time. Like an alcoholic who tries to prove he is not an alcoholic by trying to stay away from liquor for a few days, T.J. was trying to prove to herself that she was not really addicted to gambling. But she was losing the battle.

T.J. was absently rubbing suntan lotion on her already well-oiled tanned body. She heard him before saw him.

"Do you want me to do that for you?"

"John? What in the world are you...I mean, have you been on this cruise all along?"

"Actually, I just got here."

"But how...?"

"I flew."

"Oh? Why?"

"I wanted to be with you."

"But…" T.J. was about to tell John that they barely knew each other when he said softly.

"I love you."

"No. No you don't. If you knew me, really knew me, you couldn't possibly love me."

"I know all I need to know. I just spent two hours with your mother and aunts."

"You what? Forget it, I don't want to know."

"It's as if I've been looking for you all my life and suddenly, here you are. You will never know how meeting you has changed my life."

"John, I'm a gambler. I lose money. I hurt people, even those I love. I lie to everyone to cover my addiction. I even escaped from a psychiatric hospital Monday morning."

John laughed. "You did? Well, in that case, I love you even more."

T.J. laughed with him. "You do?"

"Let me do that," John said, reaching for the bottle of suntan lotion. "Turn over."

John massaged the lotion into T.J.'s neck and shoulders slowly. She was the first woman he'd touched intimately in a long while, and he was surprised when he became quickly aroused.

T.J. felt her muscles relax as his gentle hands moved lightly over her body. She also felt an unexpected sexual stirring that frightened her a little.

"Let's talk, OK?"

"Talk," John said huskily, his hands continuing on their magical path down T.J.'s smooth back.

T.J. could feel the heat from his touch radiate all through her body. She sat up quickly and started to protest that she was not ready for this. Her life was too screwed up. She didn't need complications. Instead, she found herself in John's arms. He was kissing her. They were kissing each other. Not the sweet, chaste kiss like the one they shared the night they went to the casino, but one filled with passion and an incredible yearning for more.

"I am finally gonna do it," T.J. told herself. She wanted to go to bed with Mr. John Conti more than she had ever wanted anything in her whole life. Now!

"Whoa," she said instead. "I thought we were going to talk."

And they did. For three days. They talked. They kissed. They talked more. They sipped Merlot. They went to dinner. They slow danced, their bodies moving as one, to music they didn't really hear. They talked some more.

T.J. told John everything. John was good at listening. He had been taught as a child born into the Family how to hear everything by saying nothing. But he listened because he wanted to help T.J. He wanted to make her happy. To take her load of problems and carry them for her.

"I know some people in Gamblers Anonymous. You get some help and I'll pay off this Deluca character. OK?"

T.J. didn't tell John that Angelo had already agreed to wipe out the debt if she spied on him. For some reason, she didn't reveal Angelo's interest in him nor her desperate agreement to help Angelo find out whatever he was trying to find out about him.

John found himself being candid for the first time in his life about what it was like growing up in a Mafia family. He told her about his mother's secret efforts to steer him away from the violent and criminal aspects of his father's world. How she had convinced his father to send him to Harvard. Since the Family had been going legitimate for years,

John's father readily agreed. He had big plans for his only child. A smart, young attorney for a son could be a real asset in presenting a clean face to the world. So John would help manage the Family's multi-million dollar businesses and take over when the time was right.

John didn't tell T.J. what happened when his father's long-time bodyguard, Bobby "Bigfoot" Farollo caught him and Winston Avery, III, one of his fraternity brothers in the cabana on his parent's modest estate in Jersey.

"What's wrong?" T.J. asked, noticing the dark look that had come suddenly to him. "I think it's wonderful that you grew up in that environment without becoming involved in the dirt."

"Nothing's wrong. I just haven't touched you in the past five minutes and I need to touch you. Really touch you."

"I know," T.J. murmured, moving into his arms once again.

T.J. returned his kisses with a passion she had never felt before.

"Your cabin or mine?" they asked in unison.

"Mine," they both replied.

           *   *   *

Michael Zello had learned from the informant in Lake Charles that John Conti and Jimmy Addolina were lovers. But the guy could tell him nothing about Conti's involvement in the Mafia or the gambling industry in Louisiana.

Michael sped back to New Orleans. He couldn't wait to share this information about Conti with T.J. Obviously, Mr. Harvard graduate Mafia man wasn't a competitor for T.J.'s affections as he had originally thought.

Yet he was no further along in locating and dealing with the Mafia connection to gaming in the State. He still thought Conti was heading the Mob's gambling interests in Louisiana. But whoever heard of a gay Mafiosa? Maybe Conti was only pretending to be gay, so no one would suspect the truth. Michael was beginning to confuse himself.

The only thing he knew for sure was he missed T.J. and couldn't wait to see her again.

When Michael returned to New Orleans, he was disappointed to learn that T.J. had disappeared. He called Diana who reluctantly told him about the Greek cruise. She was obviously not inclined to have a clumsy fisherman become a member of her family. Michael already knew T.J. was not on the Greek cruise.

He tried her office and was told that she was on vacation. Twice he'd seen her in the Quarter with a young woman. He shouldn't have trouble finding out her name. After all, he was FBI.

*   *   *

T.J. wasted no time getting out of the little black dress. So, this is love she thought as she squeezed into the small berth with an equally enthusiastic and gorgeously naked John Conti.

They were so compatible, intellectually, emotionally, and, she hoped, sexually. Yeah.

"T.J., I need to tell you something before we do this."

"What? Don't tell me you're a virgin, too?"

"Too? You're- No, I'm not exactly a virgin, I'm…"

Before John could say another word, the door to the stateroom was flung open and a man with a brown paper bag over his head appeared. The eyes and mouth were cut out like a jack-o-lantern and the word "ain'ts" was written on it. The intruder pulled a huge gun out of his belt and aimed it at the couple.

"This here's a bugery."

"Oh, my God," T.J. whispered, "I'm going to die a virgin."

"Get up and put yo clothes on," the gunman ordered.

Both John and T.J. rose quickly to obey the command.

"Not you, John. And turn your head around. I don't want you to watch her gettin dressed."

"Jimmy?"

"You know the robber?"

"I ain't no robber, Missy. I'm his lover."

John glared at Jimmy. Jimmy glared at T.J. T.J. glared at John.

"Get out!" they shouted at each other.

Jimmy headed for the door, the Saint's bag still over his head. T.J., dress askew, followed. She glanced back at John, who was pulling his pants up hurriedly.

"Let me explain. You can't go," John said quietly.

"Well, just watch me, you S.O.B." T.J. stepped out quickly only to return a second later. She moved aside as John eased past her.

"Your cabin," he said.

"Yes, my cabin," she muttered, tears streaming down her face.

*   *   *

The Checker cab driver watched as T.J. left the cruise ship, then stepped hurriedly toward her. She was practically racing off the ship, looking back over her shoulder as if the devil was in close pursuit.

He shouted "cab here" to get her attention, then opened the rear door for her. An elderly couple arrayed in island greens and yellows stepped in.

"I'm sorry, this taxi's taken," the driver said, watching T.J. approach.

"I don't see anybody in here, young fellow," the woman objected.

"Look, I just got a bomb threat. Somebody's out to get all the cab drivers in New Orleans. You don't have much time."

The couple moved faster than they had in years to vacate the taxi. They were taken back when the young cabbie with his Elvis-type sideburns grabbed the pretty gal who almost ran them down in her haste to take their place. Then, instead of telling the girl about his cab being ready to blow, he started kissing her. All over. The couple had never seen such impudence, and were about to come to the defense of the surprised newcomer, when she said with a puzzled look on her face, "Angelo?"

"Get in."

"Are you nuts? I don't need this right now."

"What? Get in the taxi. I just want to take you home. We need to talk. OK?"

T.J. looked back and saw John approaching. Jimmy was nowhere in sight.

"Let's go," she said, jumping in the back seat and dragging her suitcase in with her.

The couple watched in amazement as the cabbie named Angelo hopped in after her, then took off like he was some kind of race car driver. They stood with open mouths as another young fellow approached, moved them away from a second taxi they were about to enter and told the driver to "follow that cab". Just like in the movies. The old fellow shook his head, mumbling something about how they should have stayed off the ship if they wanted excitement.

Chapter 7

The Wisest Guy

The place where the group was meeting was across the Lake on Rigolets Road. It was a run-down, deserted looking building on stilts that once housed one of the best seafood restaurants in the Slidell area. People would flock in from New Orleans on Friday nights to savor its boiled crabs and shrimp, the giant fried seafood platters, delicious soft-shelled crab and crispy bayou catfish. Until an IRS notice appeared on the front door. A lien for non-payment of back taxes. It never reopened to the public. It was an ideal place for a secret meeting.

"I want to know who this Angelo Deluca is."

"But, Boss, you gotta give my man some time to get the lowdown on him. He's…"

"No. No more time. I want to know everything about him, including what color his pee is. Now. Is that clear, Frankie?"

"Yeah." Frank Modella looked down. In fact, the other ten did the same. The young man addressing the group was angry and the old-timers didn't want to be the recipient of his wrath.

"What do you know so far?"

"Small time punk shark. From the Nort somewhere. Been around a couple-a-years. On his own. Keeps out of our way. Not interested in the games."

"Yeah, then why's he asking so many questions?"

"No one told me he's been noseying around."

"Well, I'm telling you. Find out why."

"Sure, Boss. Anything you say."

The young man faced the group. These men hadn't had real leadership in years and were hungry for someone to tell them what to do. They were good men, loyal. But getting on in age. The gambling industry's debut in Louisiana had revived their spirits.

They had come alive with the excitement of being back in action. But they were old and rusty. He wasn't sure he could depend on them as much as his **padrino** had.

"Any word on what the Feds are up to?"

"Nay. They think we're all dead or senile or something," Joseph Romano spoke up. Joey looked like he was on his last leg, but his mind was still sharp even though he was in his late eighties.

"Actually, I heard they've concentrated all their efforts in getting the goods on psychiatric hospitals. Medicare and health care fraud. They're even putting plants in those places. Posing as bookkeepers and such."

Everyone laughed at Johnnie Salvatori's tidbit on the FBI. Except the leader of the group. He rarely laughed in their presence. Wanted to keep them on their toes. Although he frowned upon all that hand-kissing crap, he still insisted they show him the proper respect by calling him boss and jumping to his commands. So he stared at each one 'til the laughter died down.

"What's the take, Phil?"

"We did a little better this month. Couple of weak spots, but I got Lou on them. I'll have last month's books closed in a few days. But no surprises."

Phil Sacco looked up, hoping for a word or two of praise and getting a scowl instead.

"Good, cause I hate surprises."

Things had not been going well for the gambling industry in Louisiana for a while now. First, there were a bunch of arrests because a few Family members from New York got caught in the Video Poker Scandal of '95. Then it was rumored that a pile of legislators was being bought off for their votes. And in '96, the good people of Louisiana elected a new governor who wasn't overly fond of gambling and had been trying ever since to get each parish to vote it out. Thus, an uneasiness about their operation always prevailed in the weekly meetings.

"OK, everyone. When we meet again next time, I expect to have the scoop on that Deluca character. That's it for tonight."

Long after the others had gone, the young Don set sipping a glass of wine. His thoughts were on T.J. He was determined to marry her. He loved her. Really loved her. He knew she loved him. She just didn't realize how much. He would show her.

Chapter 8

Dating Games I

The Neville Brothers minus Aaron was expected to begin playing shortly and the House of Blues on Decatur was bustling. T.J. was relaxed despite the smoky, loud atmosphere inside the popular club. She watched Angelo as he nursed his wine. Neither tried to talk over the din, and that was fine with T.J.

They had made a shaky peace of sorts following the wild cab ride back to her apartment after she had invited him in. Actually, he had invited himself in and she had been too heartbroken to argue. She had tried in vain to hold back the tears, but was soon sobbing uncontrollably. Michael had stood helplessly for a moment or so, before taking her in his arms. Although he had whispered over and over that "it was going to be Ok," he didn't know for sure what "it" was.

T.J. had been too embarrassed to talk about what had happened with John, and Michael had lost his desire to gloat over his own discovery concerning Conti and Addolina. Instead he had guided T.J. to the sofa and held her until she fell asleep. He then let himself out of the apartment without awakening her and had called her the next day to arrange the Friday night date.

So here they were. And T.J. was glad the noise kept her from having to explain what had occurred on the cruise ship.

In the early morning hours, they walked arm in arm back to her apartment on Conti Street. Michael broke the silence.

"I'm sorry about the DePaul thing. I was pissed because you lied to me about going on that Greek cruise. I didn't mean to hurt you, you know."

"I know, Angelo. It's just that I was so upset about being there. I mean, I needed to be there, but it's a long story."

"Whenever you're ready, I'm here. OK?"

"You know for a...I mean, you're really a nice guy."

"For a what?"

"Nothing. I need to apologize to you, too."

"For what?"

"For carrying on like such a baby the other night."

"I love bambinos."

T.J. laughed. As they approached her apartment, they became quiet. For someone who in the past had never even bothered to ask before practically smothering her with his kisses, Michael was almost shy as he brought his face close to hers.

"Friends?" T.J. asked, holding out her hand.

"Sure," Michael said, ignoring her hand and moving hurriedly off into the night without even saying goodbye.

I really had a good time, T.J. thought as she let herself into her apartment. Too bad Angelo was a mobster. She knew he wanted to kiss her and was kind of wishing he had not given up so easily. But it was best that she had not allowed it. Because after the fiasco with John on the ship, she was never going to open herself up to anyone again. Especially someone like Angelo Deluca. In fact she was never going to let anyone hurt her again. To hell with love.

         *   *   *

Despite her resolve not to leave herself exposed to the pain of a romantic relationship, she accepted a date with John the very next day.

"I don't want to talk to you," she said firmly when he called. And meant it. At first.

"You don't have to talk. I'll talk. Just have dinner with me. I made reservations at La Louisiane for tonight."

It was almost a command and T.J. was tempted to tell him where to get off. But he had managed to make her fall in love with him and she wanted to see him. She needed to see him.

"OK. What time?"

"I'll pick you up at seven o'clock."

T.J. took more care with her appearance than she ever had in her entire life. She wore a very short, red silk no-name dress that clung to her lithe body. "I'll make him regret the day he even heard the word, gay," she mumbled to the mirror.

La Louisiane had been around forever and was a favorite dining spot for tourists in the Quarter. But locals, too, especially young couples, flocked to the restaurant because of its romantic ambiance.

T.J. and John both ordered the soft shell crab for which the restaurant was quickly becoming famous. They had made only polite conversation since they left her apartment and T.J. was starting to feel uncomfortable.

"This is good," She said, not able to look at John directly.

"You know, I meant it when I said I love you."

"I don't want to hear this. I have lots of gay friends. Gay is gay. I hate that you were going to use me to as a cover or whatever you were trying to do. I just don't want to hear your lies."

T.J.'s words were not spoken in anger. She just didn't want to be hurt any more by this man she had fallen in love with.

"Look, I'll admit I was looking for someone to, to, well, for a woman. But I didn't count on falling in love with you. We can make this work. Lots of gay men marry, have families, you know."

"John, I love you. I really do. But, I could never marry you. I'm Italian. I'm very possessive and jealous. I couldn't even handle your looking at another woman. Can you imagine what would happen if I caught you with another man?"

"That would never happen. I would never let it happen. Honor is everything. I'd never go back on my word."

"Oh, great. You'd stick by me even if you fell in love with some guy because you'd feel obligated," T.J. said loudly.

The approaching young waiter overheard T.J. and backed away before they noticed him, obviously deciding this was not a good time to ask them if everything was OK.

The conversation became even more intense during cappucino and sinfully delicious bread pudding. John told T.J. that he was not going to give up trying to win her back. He was going to marry her and that was that.

By the time they got back to her apartment, all T.J. wanted to do was rip off his clothes and drag him to her four-poster bed and jump his bones. Yes, rape him. Then she thought sadly, that's just what she would be doing. Raping him. She loved him too much for that. She accepted his swift, hard kiss and told him somewhat breathlessly that, yes, it would be OK if he called.

"Friends?" T.J. asked offering him her hand.

"Sure." He brought her hand to his mouth and sucked the tip of her ring finger without taking his eyes off her. Then his face broke out in a rare, gorgeous grin and he waved goodbye.

*   *   *

On Sunday, Steve called from Tallula, asking if she was going to be free in the afternoon, since he was coming to New Orleans and needed to talk with her. She and Lawanna had been planning to attend a crawfish boil at a mutual friend's loft apartment on Magazine Street. Steve said he hadn't had good boiled crawfish in ages and would love to join them if she didn't mind. They planned to meet at her apartment about 3 p.m.

T.J. was telling Lawanna about how she found out John was gay. Both young women had tears streaming down their faces. T.J.'s tears were caused by the greatest heartbreak she'd ever known. Her friend's were the result of uncontrollable laughter as she listened to T.J.'s weird story.

"What do you mean, his lover broke into your cabin wearing a grocery bag over his head?"

"Not a grocery sack, it was one of those old Saints bags that the fans used to wear when the Saints lost all the time," T.J. countered indignantly, then started laughing herself.

"Then you actually had a date with this jerk and you let him suck your finger?"

"Well, yes. I mean no. I was trying to shake hands with him and he just grabbed my finger and started sucking on it."

"And?"

"And, I would have let him suck all of my fingers and toes and anything else if he had wanted, but…"

"Girl, you are crazy. Pure-dee-crazy," Lawanna managed. She was laughing so hard now, she actually plopped from the sofa onto the floor. She was lying there, laughing hysterically when the doorbell rang.

T.J., in complete agreement with Lawanna's assessment of her mental state, started bawling anew. She was nuts.

The doorbell rang again. After a while it was opened and Steve Rose was greeted by a distressed looking T.J. with a pitiful fake smile on her face that was still streaked by tears.

"What's wrong with her?" Steve asked, pointing to Lawanna who was trying to sit up, but started laughing again and had to lie back down.

T.J. looked at Lawanna and just dismissed her with a wave.

"Hello? What's going on here?"

"I'm sorry, Steve. Give me a moment, please. We'll talk later.
OK?" T.J. walked to the bedroom and closed the door behind her. She
could be heard shouting something about how she should have just
stayed in the loony bin with all the old people and let the bastards
give her electric shock treatment because that wouldn't have hurt at
all compared to this.

Lawanna, almost recovered now, took one look at the puzzled look
on Steve's face and started howling again. She wasn't the least bit
guilty about being the one who told John Conti where he could find T.J.
in the first place.

            *   *   *

The apartment belonged to two young artists who had converted the
old warehouse to a showplace filled with special touches like hand-
painted walls and ceilings. It was a massive one-room apartment filled
with skillfully refinished antiques found in the few junk shops that still
existed on Magazine Street.

Pounds and pounds of steaming crawfish were spread out on newspaper on a round table huge enough to seat twenty people if necessary.
The table was situated under a modern painting splashed with bright
orange and yellow. The room as well as the mood of the dozen or so
young people was cheerful. The guests stuffed themselves with the
tasty delicacy, corn-on-the-cob and new potatoes that had all been
boiled in the same massive pot.

T.J. found her spirits lifting and she joined in as her friends discussed
the latest movies, the city's new mayor, who was appearing at the local
clubs. Lawanna had latched on to a good-looking, unattached young
architect and had moved from the table to an oak trundle bed that was
used as a loveseat companion to a plush sofa.

T.J. and Steve took their beers and sat side by side on a cushioned
window seat that overlooked Magazine. It started to rain and lulled by

the steady beat on the metal roof, T.J. placed her head on her soulmate's shoulder and almost dozed.

"Are you feeling better now?"

"Much. I forgot how just being with you makes everything all right. Steve, I can't really talk about what's been happening right now. I need to sort it all out first. OK?"

"You used to be able to tell me anything. I want it to be that way again."

"In that case, seen Sister lately?"

"No, in fact, I'm not seeing Mary Jane socially anymore?"

"Oh? Why not?"

"I'm in love with someone else."

"Oh?" Despite everything, the thought of Steve being serious about anyone still bothered her."

"What about you? Seen Sister lately?"

"Almost. Almost," T.J. answered sadly.

Steve didn't know what happened, but he was sure it had something to do with John Conti. He had tried to warn T.J. about him, but she obviously hadn't listened. She never did.

"T.J., when are you coming home again?"

"Home? My home is here. In New Orleans."

"Would you ever consider moving back to Tallula?"

"I don't think I could ever go back...to live. My job is here. My friends are here. Except for you. Besides, I love New Orleans."

"And I love you."

"I know. And I love you, too, but I'm staying here."

T.J. was upset by the frown that suddenly appeared on Steve's face. "Are we still friends?" she asked.

"T.J., I want us to be more than friends. I want us to get married. Settle down and have a bunch of children. I really love you."

"You're serious," T.J. said softly.

Steve was about to show T.J. just how serious he was when Lawanna appeared.

"You guys having fun?"

"Yes, Doctor Lewis," Steve answered. "Now, go away so we can have more fun."

"T.J., why's your mouth open?"

"Uh, Steve was just telling me a joke."

"You want to share it?"

"Yes, but later. Right now, I just want to go home. I have to go back to work tomorrow and I need to regroup and all."

"Well, I'm going to hang around a bit longer," Lawanna smiled in the direction of the young architect. "I'll call you later."

By the time T.J. and Steve got back to the apartment, he had been paged twice. He stayed long enough to call his service.

"I need to head back to Tallula right away. Will you think about what I've said?"

"Of course. I don't know what to say. But, I'll be visiting my parents next weekend. We can talk some more then. OK?"

"OK," Steve said. He gave T.J. a long, passionate kiss, then left without another word.

T.J. thought about what being Steve's wife would be like. She'd have to give up her job and her beloved New Orleans because she knew he'd never leave Tallula. She didn't know if she could do that for any man.

Besides, she had every intention of joining one of the many Gamblers Anonymous groups in New Orleans. Even if St. Mary Parish had a couple of groups, she didn't want her family to know about her problem. Just yet. She would tell them when and if it was no longer a problem. She hadn't gambled since Charenton and her first date with John, but that didn't mean anything.

John. The real reason she didn't want to decide about Steve's proposal. She loved Stephen Rose. Always had. But she was in love with John. As hopeless as the situation with him was. She couldn't help how she felt about him.

T.J. played back messages on the answering machine from her Mom and Angelo asking her to call them. She pulled a bottle of Evian water out of her refrigerator, thinking about her three weekend dates. Suddenly she smiled. "Well, I may be the only twenty-seven-year-old virgin in the City, but I'm definitely the most proposed-to one," she told herself. "And by far, the most well-kissed one."

Chapter 9
Doc's Diagnosis

The Tallula City Council held its monthly meeting in the KC Hall on Main Street. The Knights of Columbus was still an active organization, and since Tony was the town's mayor as well as the KC's Grand Knight, meeting in the Hall made sense.

Tony glanced around the large room before calling the meeting to order. All seven of the Council members were present. They were seated at a school cafeteria table facing about seventy-five metal folding chairs being quickly filled.

Father Hebert sat next to Lou Ella Turner who had given up cigarettes when the High School adopted a smoke-free environment a few years back. At the moment, she was elbowing L.J. La Deaux in an effort to get him to put out his cigarette. Father Hebert leaned across Lou Ella trying desperately to get a whiff of it.

Millie Washington was telling Tom Walters that the grass in the small city park wasn't being cut regularly enough. Miss Emmie agreed and said she would bring it up even though it wasn't on the agenda. Doc Romero, the seventh Council member seated at the table, seemed preoccupied and was quieter than usual tonight.

Turnout for town meetings was usually good, and tonight was no exception. Every chair was taken. Word had it that the Council was going to recommend some sort of formal tax protest, and although rumors of this sort weren't new, having the City Council seriously consider the possibility of a tax revolt was. So by the time Tony called the meeting to order, the room bristled with tension and excitement.

"Miss Emmie, would you read the minutes from the last meeting?"

It took the postmistress a good fifteen minutes to read her one page of scribbled notes and people were sighing and coughing and finally before she even finished, someone in the back row yelled that he moved that the minutes be approved. The motion was quickly seconded by about thirty people.

Then, Millie Washington gave the treasurer's report and got a unified groan when she announced the town's two CDs were now earning only 5.2% interest.

The only old business was a report on the status of the new pet ordinance. Dogs and cats had always roamed freely in Tallula until Emelda Walters sicked her Pit Bull on the encyclopedia salesman from Morgan City when he woke her from her daily nap. He had to have a bunch of stitches.

Although the whole incident didn't have a thing to do with the dog being on the loose, the Council thought it best to at least have a leash law on the books. Because the salesman had threatened to sue the City as well as Emelda. Nothing had come of it so far, but rumor had it that the fellow had a habit of purposely pushing his wares a bit too hard. So, it wasn't the first job-related bite he had received and it wouldn't be the last. He lived on the proceeds from his lawsuits and not on his meager earnings from the rare sale of his books. The pain he endured from the self-provoked attacks by man and beast alike was obviously well worth it.

Miss Emmie, feeling the crowd's impatience with her earlier presentation, decided not to bring up the grass-cutting problem. So soon a heated discussion on the pros and cons of a tax protest and the form it should take ensued.

Almost a month had passed since April 15 and the people tended to forget their anger at the government for taking so much of their hard-earned money. Even though there were constant reminders from the media.

It was announced just today in the Baton Rouge Morning Advocate that taxpayers were now working a whole extra week for the government. All the way to May, in fact.

Tom Walters was responding to a question by Julius Green on the legal repercussions of not filing.

"Actually, if you don't file, it's only a misdemeanor. Now, if you falsify a return, then that's a felony. So, we have to be careful about how we choose to let those sons-of-bitches in Washington know we're not happy about the tax system," Tom shouted at old Julius.

Tom glanced at Viola Perkins to see if she was smiling approval of his expertise on tax law. All heads in the room turned toward Tom's lover in unison. All except Emelda, that is. She was busy voicing disapproval of Diana Marino's new Kathie Lee hairstyle to Lena La Deaux. Meanwhile, Diana, flanked by two of The Sisters, Frances and Annie, all three fanning in unison, challenged the lawyer angrily.

"Yeah, but Tom, haven't they recently made it easier on us. You know, putting the burden of proof on themselves. And letting us sue them if they do us wrong?" she asked.

Tony was tempted to respond for Tom, but he and Diana had been fighting again. Since she'd walked in on him and his secretary the other day. Although, Jenny Breaux was nothing to write home about, she was a good fifteen years younger than Diana who was by her Italian nature insanely jealous to start with.

Diana had decided to surprise Tony with an old fashioned picnic lunch. Jenny was not at her desk so Diana had charged into Tony's office. Tony was seated at his desk and Jenny was standing behind him massaging his shoulders. Diana had flung the basket at them, scattering biscuits and Popeyes fried chicken all over the place. Despite Tony's vehement denial that there was anything going on between him and

Jenny and his half-hearted offer to fire her, Diana hadn't spoken to him since. So he was not about to put his two cents in now. He let Tom continue instead.

"Well, actually, we were thrown a few election year crumbs, but the system still burdens most Americans," Tom said to Diana and sparking a lively debate in the Hall.

The discussion went back and forth for an hour or so before Doc Romero spoke up.

"The trouble with us," he said in a soft voice that barely hinted of a Spanish accent, "is we are all suffering from the April 15 syndrome."

Although not one person understood what he meant, nobody questioned that he knew what he was talking about. Roberto Romero had been brought over from Mexico by his uncle, Doctor Jose Jimenez, as soon as he'd graduated from medical school over 40 years ago. No one knew how it came about that Dr. Jimenez had settled in the small southern town because he didn't speak a word of English.

Never-the-less, the people took to Doctor Jimenez immediately. They never learned exactly what ailed them since none understood Spanish. But since Dr. Jimenez always made them feel better, they figured it didn't really matter. As long as he could cure them, they flocked to his office.

Until the day Dr. Jimenez died, most of his patients still couldn't decipher the few proudly acquired words of heavily-accented English that laced his Spanish. But they loved him. And they loved his nephew even more because they could understand what he was saying. Usually.

"The April 15 syndrome," Doc Romero repeated. "Every year the symptoms are the same. Anger, depression, irritability, overindulgence to ease the pain and an unhealthy desire to regain control of our finances. Paying taxes makes us all a little crazy. For a while even your best friends and closest neighbors are not who you think they are. In fact, nothing is what it seems to be."

The townspeople murmured to each other. "What's he talking about?" "Doc's a little down tonight, don't you think?" "I knew Doc was gonna finally flip, too much pressure you know."

Finally, Tony who had lost control of the meeting, if he ever had it, called for order, before turning to the physician.

"Are you saying we need to forget making a formal protest?" Tony asked, somewhat perturbed by his friend's desertion to the side of reason.

"I'm just saying that we ought to give ourselves time to heal. A few months. Then if we decide to protest as a town by not filing our individual taxes next year, we'll be making a decision based on conviction and not the syndrome. Understand?"

Doc Romero's advice led to a motion to table the tax protest matter for a few months. Most everyone was disappointed and very relieved.

Tony asked if there was any more new business and was about to adjoin the meeting when Cora Johnson decided to make her presence known.

"I think we need to end this meeting with a prayer. There are a lot of sinners in this place and..."

"Cora, this is not a church," Tony started to say, then realizing that Diana had told Cora about their fight and just might share the reason for it with everyone here, relented.

"Father, would you lead us in prayer, please?"

Father Hebert stood up. Made the sign of the cross. Everyone, even the two Jewish couples who had lived in the predominantly Catholic town forever, made the sign of the cross. Lana Rosenberg always clutched her Star of David broach and made the sign with crossed fingers just in case.

"Dear God," Father Hebert began, "please forgive the sinners here tonight. The adulterers..." All three of The Sisters and Cora looked at Tony. Everyone else looked at Tom and Viola who were looking at each other. "The liars." Everyone looked around to see who was looking uncomfortable. "The gamblers." Everyone looked at everyone else. Cora Johnson just glared at the little priest. "The alcoholics." Lots of the townspeople drank, some heavily, so most were looking at their shoes. "The gossipers." Emelda took the brunt of the self-righteous stares.

Father Hebert glanced around the room thinking that his prayers should have taken care of just about everyone here tonight. Then he spotted Frankie Colarossi standing in the back of the Hall with two of his goons. "And of course, the contractors." Everyone looked at Julius who had made a lot of people unhappy with his numerous construction delays over the years. Frankie Colarossi had the faintest of smiles on his face. He and Henry Hebert went back many years. The jovial priest was one of the few people around who could get away with joking at the ancient Don's expense and live to be an old man.

The meeting adjourned with no plans to revolt. But with a very real anti-tax sentiment that was not going to die easily.

Everyone seemed reluctant to go home and many were milling around greeting each other like long lost friends despite the fact they saw each other daily for the most part.

Tony broke from Tom Walters and Lou Ella Turner and headed for Diana who was telling a group of ladies that T.J. was acting very mysteriously lately and that could mean only one thing. Wedding bells. She hoped.

Diana saw her husband approaching and headed abruptly out the door, startling the women who stared after her with mouths agape. As Tony sped past her in hot pursuit of his wife, Cora shouted to him in a voice loud enough for everyone to hear.

"The good Lord is gonna punish you for the hurt you put on that poor woman."

Cora stayed for another twenty minutes or so telling everyone who would listen that Miz Marino had caught the Mayor and his "secatary" carrying on right there in Town Hall. When they asked for specifics, she just said, "The good Lord could strike me down dead for even thinking about what they was doing."

Cora couldn't wait to get back to Fair Oaks for the next angry episode between her employers. She was glad T.J. would be home in few days so she could fill her in on the latest spat going on at home and all that nonsense about tax protests. Diana and Tony never told T.J. the whole truth about anything. Still treated her like a baby. Always trying to protect their only daughter. So, it was usually left up to her to set that child straight. She couldn't wait to do her God-given duty.

Chapter 10

All In La Familia

John Conti entered his Grandpa's house on the River through the kitchen. He nodded to the two "soldiers" always stationed outside this entrance and knocked a couple of times, so as not to startle Rosalie. Frankie's longtime housekeeper never failed to invite him to sit down at the white-clothed table and sample whatever delicacy she happened to be creating at the time. And Rosalie, always clad in the traditional black of a Sicilian widow despite never being married, was a marvelous cook.

This time John brushed off her invitation to sit by planting a kiss on the tiny woman's forehead. He grabbed a fresh-out-of-the-oven Italian fig cookie as he headed down the hall.

"Is he in his study?" John asked stuffing the whole cookie in his mouth and not waiting for an answer.

The door to Frankie's study was open, so John walked in. Frankie was seated behind a massive mahogany desk. If it weren't for the several pillows that he thought no one knew about, all you would see as you sat opposite him would be his head. Frankie still expected the respectful hand kiss and John was more than happy to comply. After all, his Grandfather had taken the news of his homosexuality rather well and was doing all he could to turn his grandson around. So John knew he'd want to help him.

It was just early afternoon, but the room was too dark to really see much of anything. The old Don liked it that way.

"Paw-Paw, I need a favor from you."

"Well, Johnnie, you've come to the right place. Whatcha need?"

"I'm in love and I want to get married."

"Is it a...?"

"A woman?"

"I did'n know," Frankie raised both shoulders in a shirk.

"Well, she is a woman. A wonderful woman. And I love her more than anything."

"Then, what'sa problem? She's not...?"

"Gay?"

"I did'n know." He shirked again.

"No, she's not gay, but she found out I was. Used to be?"

"How?"

"A friend of mine told her and now she won't marry me because she doesn't think I can change."

"Whatcha want me to do?"

"Just tell me what you would do if you were in my shoes."

"Your shoes? Oh, you mean if I'm in love with someone who did'n love me? I'd just make her an offer she couldn't refuse."

"What kind of offer?"

"Just let me think about it. I'll get back to you."

"Thanks, Paw-Paw."

"By the way, who's dis young lady who finally turned your head in the right direction?"

"T.J. Marino."

"Ah, T.J. Marino." The old Don smiled, knowing exactly what he needed to do.

*   *   *

The young Don entered Frankie's study about thirty minutes after John Conti left. He, too, deferred to his mentor by kissing the old man's hand.

"**Parran**, I need your help."

Frankie glanced at his successor whose face looked ominous in the eerie darkness. He was proud of the way he was handling the business in South Louisiana.

"What's wrong?" Frankie asked, knowing that his Godson was not having an easy time maintaining control of the Family's gambling interests lately. It wasn't like in the old days when you could just buy off a few people or just plain off them if they got in your way.

Despite the Sicilian Mob's supposed demise in this country, the Feds still milked their victory over their ancient enemy for every thing it was worth. Any hint of the Mafia's resurfacing was squashed immediately. And Frankie knew the FBI was watching Louisiana gaming very carefully.

"It's not business. It's personal."

"Personal?" Frankie asked, thinking his Godson had never asked for his help before. Even the time, he got picked up by Sheriff Washington for driving 100 miles an hour through town at 3 a.m. when he was just thirteen years old. The teenager had begged the sheriff not to tell a soul. Promised the man he'd repay the favor some day. Frankie had learned of the incident years later. That's when he knew who his heir to the business was going to be.

"I'm waiting."

"I'm in love and I want to get married."

"But that's wonderful. A man needs a wife. A family. We'll have a big wedding."

"There's a problem. Two problems really."

"What? What problem?"

"I haven't told her about all this," he said, indicating the dark room as if it alone stood for his hidden sinister side.

"Then, don't tell her."

"I have to tell her. Don't you think she's going to wonder why I'm hanging out with strange old hoods several times a week? How did you handle it? What did you tell **Nanan**?"

"I did'n tell Lucia nothing. I did'n have to. In those days, women don't ask. They just did what they was told. Kept their mouths shut. Baked bread."

"Well, not today. And certainly not T.J."

"T.J.? Tony and Diana Marino's girl?"

"Yes. You sound surprised."

"I'm not surprised. What'sya other problem? You said there was two."

"I don't think she wants to marry me."

"There's someone else. I mean, there's someone else?"

"Why do you think that?"

"I did'n know," the old Don shrugged, "I'm just asking. What do you want me to do?"

"I'm not really sure. I guess I just wanted to talk with you about it. But if you can think of anything to help me win her over, I'll be indebted to you for the rest of my life."

"You are indebted to me for the rest of your life. And beyond," Frankie said remembering how after he had ordered the hit on his Godchild's father, he personally took the small boy under his protective wing. No one could say Frankie Colarossi was not an honorable man. "I'll see what I can do", he said.

"Thanks, **Parran**."

Frankie sat alone for a few moments thinking about the crazy love triangle his Godson and grandson and this Marino woman were in. Then he started laughing. He laughed so hard Rosalie came running to see what was wrong. Frankie reassured her that nothing was the matter and asked her to bring him one of those delicious fig cookies Johnnie was eating earlier.

Frankie picked up the phone, but hesitated before dialing. He had used Jimmy Addolina a couple of times in the past. The man was an idiot, but he should be able to handle arranging a little meeting between him and Miss Marino. He started laughing again as he called Addolina. Frankie had no idea that the man was his grandson's ex-lover.

*   *   *

Jimmy was scared to death as he grabbed the old Don's hand and began slobbering all over it. He was sure Frankie had found out about him and John and really believed he would never leave the pitch-black study alive. He tried to cover his fear with pleasant conversation, but he had to go to the john real bad.

"Your Holiness, I am so proud you invited me into your private statuary. It's beautiful," he gushed, barely able to see anything at all in the dark room.

"Do you know T.J. Marino?"

"Uh, kind of." The question surprised him.

"Kind of? You know her or you don't. Now what is it?"

If he admitted he knew her, and John had confessed everything to his grandpa, especially the boat escapade, he was a dead man. But if he denied knowing her and Frankie knew he was lying, he was even deader. Surely the old man would off him for messing around with his grandson and ruining any chance of a relationship between him and the Marino bitch. He whispered his answer as if that would save him.

"Yes, Godfather, I know the little tr..., uh, Miz Marino."

"Good, now here's what I want you to do."

Reeling with relief, Jimmy leaned against the worn leather chair. He squeezed his legs together as Frankie's plan unfolded.

*   *   *

Despite the fact that it was late Friday evening, the trip from New Orleans to Tallula didn't seem to take as long as usual. T.J. spent the time trying to figure out what she was going to say to Steve.

Why not marry her best friend? She argued with herself that although the relationship lacked the excitement she felt with John, Steve would always be there for her. Even though he had a reputation for enjoying the company and bodies of a number of women over the years, he would never hurt her.

She had always loved Steve. He was comfortable, reliable, rather wonderful. T.J. was ready for marriage. A family. She could practice law in Morgan City. So, why not marry the young doctor and settle down?

The radio was tuned to WWL and T.J. started singing along with one of her favorite old songs. "Do you know what it means to miss New Orleans..." Tears began to fall.

She was driving on a lonely dark stretch of two-lane highway between Houma and Morgan City when a car with flashing lights and siren rushed up behind her. "Shit", she mumbled, "I was probably doing about eighty miles an hour." She slowed up and pulled off on the narrow shoulder and rolled down the window.

"Git out of the car," Jimmy Addolina ordered.

Jimmy was wearing a ski mask and pointing the same oversized handgun at T.J. At first she thought it was Angelo in one of his ridiculous disguises. It didn't take her long to realize she'd been duped by Jimmy Addolina and she was furious.

"Where are we going?" T.J. ordered, angry at herself because she had let herself be tricked by this lunatic.

"Where you're gonna git what you deserved, Missy. Doncha worry, we're almost there. And that's all I'm gonna say to you. Except, he doesn't really love you, you know. It's jus he wants to please his kin people. And that's all I'm gonna say."

Jimmy continued to talk non-stop as he drove the last twenty minutes of the trip. He didn't shut up until they entered Frankie's study, now dimly lit by a tiny desk lamp that threw shadows into the old man's face that made him look downright evil.

"Thank you, Jimmy. Wait outside."

Jimmy was hoping he'd get to stay. He was dying to know what the old man intended to do with T.J.

*   *   *

"Why is it so dark in here?" T.J. asked, walking to the wall switch and flicking it. Nothing. She had never been in the old Don's house and despite the circumstances, was more curious than afraid. She knew Frankie Colarossi's reputation, but refused to be intimidated. Even though she thought maybe she should have been. After all, she couldn't forget how in **The Godfather**, Michael had his own brother killed in that little boat. And she wasn't even a relative of this old man.

"I want to know what your intentions are."

"You had that thug drag me here to ask me what my intentions are? What are you talking about? My intentions?"

"I'm talking about what you intend to do about my grandson and Godson both being in love with you. Which one are you going to marry?"

T.J. stared at the old man like he was nuts. She knew John was Frankie Colarossi's grandson. But, she hadn't known that Angelo was his Godson."

"Well, if you must know and I can't see how it's any business of yours, I'm not going to marry either one of them."

"You're not? That's not what they think. They both admit they need to win you over, but they are also both determined to marry you."

"Well, I'm not. In fact, I came home this weekend to get engaged."

"I did'n know. You did? To who."

"Stephen Rose."

"Stephen Rose?" Frankie looked confused. "But," he started to say more, then changed his mind.

"Thank you for coming," he said instead, extending his hand like he'd just had her over for a pleasant little tea and ignoring the fact that she had been brought in at gunpoint.

"That's it?"

"Yes, thank you for coming."

"One more thing. Could someone else take me back to my car?"

"You don't like Jimmy?" Frankie laughed.

"I don't like Jimmy at all."

The girl's got guts, Frankie thought. He could see why his young men wanted her. Hell, he wanted her.

"By the way, Miss Marino."

"Yes?"

"I don't suppose your Mama ever taught you how to make good Italian bread?"

Chapter 11

Steve Comes Courting

T.J. awakened with a start. She could hear her heart beating wildly. She remembered the dream and began shivering despite the stuffy bedroom. In it, Frankie Colarossi was seated on a red velvet throne, a massive crown made of iron spikes on his head. He was flanked on smaller, but otherwise identical, thrones by Angelo and John both clad in magnificent Armani suits.

Jimmy Addolina was walking down a scarlet carpeted aisle with a bride on his arm. The bride was in chains, but her silk gown was so beautiful, everyone was ooing and aahing anyway. Especially The Sisters. Mama and Daddy were both crying hysterically.

As they approached the altar, Jimmy lifted her veil to reveal a tearful T.J., wearing a diamond and emerald studded dog collar. As they approached the throne, Jimmy handed Frankie a gold covered platter, the perfect size to conceal a head. As he lifted the lid, T.J. screamed.

She had been more curious and upset than frightened about her strange encounter with Frankie Colarossi and his unusual request that she reveal her intentions about John and Angelo. The fact that he abruptly dismissed her when she said she'd be marrying Steve was weird, but that's how things had been going for her lately. What was one more step down loony lane? Yet the nightmare scared her to death.

T.J. glanced at the old alarm that had awakened her since her high school days. It was 8 a.m., and Mama and Daddy would be awake and probably already finished with breakfast.

She had decided she would not tell her parents about Steve's proposal until after they actually became engaged. She intended to accept his proposal at dinner tonight, but she had some things she needed to do before making it official.

She wanted to be established as a member of Gamblers Anonymous with her addiction to the vice well under control. She wanted to come clean with her parents about her problems and beg their forgiveness for deceiving them so much lately. She had to straighten out things with Angelo because she cared for him even though he was bad news and just a little psycho. Mr. Colarossi's Godson. Who would have guessed? And finally, she had to say goodbye to John. She wanted to be sure she was over him before making a lasting commitment to Steve.

"I suppose I'll be saying goodbye to the 'boys from the Mob' or something like that," T.J. said out loud to a startled Cora who had come up with a cup of coffee and a pile of juicy gossip.

"Oh, Cora," T.J. laughed after hearing about her parent's latest spat, "Mama and Daddy have been married forever. They love each other. I'm not in the least bit worried."

"Well, you should be. In all my born days, I ain't never seen your poor Mama so heartbroken. And him, he jus think he can have his cake and eat it, too. But, the good Lord is watching, you hear?"

"Cora, are they downstairs? I'll go down and…"

"No, honey. Your Daddy left for the office early this morning, and your Mama…"

"Office? On Saturday?"

"What do you think I've been trying to tell you," Cora said knowingly.

"Where's Mama?"

"She just left with your Aunt Francis without telling me where she was going to be. Said to tell you she'd be back later and ya'll could talk then."

"Wow, that's not like Mama at all, to leave when I'm here and not take me with her."

"I've been trying and trying to tell you. This here is serious humbug going on."

T.J. finished dressing after Cora left to fix her a "delicious breakfast." She had a whole day to kill before meeting Stephen at 7 p.m. She wasn't in the mood for visiting old school buddies. She could drive around town trying to bump into John. She could go to the casino. That thought jolted her back to reality. She pulled off the nice khakis and slipped into an old pair of warm-ups. She'd do what she always did when she wanted to be alone with her thoughts. Dig up some worms.

T.J. stared at the red cork, willing it to move. She didn't really mind that the fish weren't biting. The river was polluted and the fish inedible anyway. She relaxed against the pier's railing and closed her eyes for a moment relishing the warmth of the sun on her face and the gentle breeze that caused her cork to bobble slightly. After a while she put her earphones on and listened to her mom's James Taylor tape.

"Do you mind if I join you?"

"You've Got a Friend" had almost lulled T.J. to sleep when she heard his voice. She turned to find Angelo standing there.

"Hi," T.J. said. "Of course not. I'm happy to see you."

She realized she was indeed glad to see him again. She hadn't heard from him since their date at the House of Blues.

"What? No disguise today?" T.J. took in his trim, muscular body clad only in a white tee and jeans, thinking he looks like one of those sexy guys in the Lee jean commercials."

"Not today. It's time you get to see the real me. T.J., there's something I need to tell you."

"I already know."

"You do?"

"Yes, Mr. Colarossi told me?"

"He knows?"

"Of course he knows. What are you talking about?"

"What are you talking about?"

"I'm talking about an invitation to meet with old man Colarossi that I couldn't refuse. I saw him last night and he wanted to know whether I was serious about his grandson or his Godson."

"And?"

"And I told him neither. I informed him of my intentions to accept Steve Rose's proposal this evening."

"What does all this have to do with my...wait a minute, you're going to marry Stephen Rose?" Michael forgot for a moment how disturbing it was to know that his cover was blown and the old Don knew he was with the Bureau. All he knew was he loved T.J. and no one was going to have her but himself.

"You can't marry Steve Rose."

"And, why not?"

"Because you don't love him."

"I've loved him all my life."

"Well, you're not in love with him."

"You don't know a damn thing about me."

"I know more than you think."

"Yeah. Like what?"

"I know you're afraid to make any kind of real commitment. Unless maybe with some gay guy who can't hurt you."

"That's ridiculous. I would have gone to bed with John in a flash if..."

"So that's it. I'll be damned. You're afraid of sex."

T.J. was furious. She dropped the cane fishing pool and hurried toward the house. Michael, realizing that once again he'd gone too far, ran after her. T.J. brushed past a startled Cora and dashed upstairs to her room.

Cora was not surprised to see a young man in hot pursuit. She lifted her eyes toward the twelve-foot ceiling and prayed. "Lord, the folk in this house sorely need your help. So if you see fit, take pity on them, even if they are Catholics."

T.J. stood at the window, tears streaming down her face. Michael entered the room without knocking and stood behind her. She turned to face him and before either one realized what was happening, they were kissing. Clothes were flung wherever and they were exploring each other's naked bodies. Soon, the groans were so loud, T.J. wondered briefly if the door was locked because she expected Cora to come charging in at any moment to save her. After a while, T.J. didn't care. This was so wonderful, all she could do was abandon herself to the miracle of love making. When it was over, she was afraid to look at Angelo. She had given up her virginity to a Mafia hood. And she had loved it. She had given up her virginity to a man she could never marry. Marry. She had given up her virginity on the day she was going to become engaged. And, not to her fiance. Where was Sister when she really needed her?

T.J. unwrapped Angelo's arm and draped in her sheet, gathered her clothes.

"You need to go now," she said, then stepped into her small bathroom to dress.

Angelo pulled his clothes on and sat in T.J.'s Bentwood rocker and waited for her to re-emerge. He glanced around T.J.'s bedroom, becoming aroused again as he took in the old metal bed now stripped of its floral top sheet. He really hadn't expected this to happen, but now that it had, he couldn't get over the wonder of it. He was no novice in the bedroom, but what he had just experienced wasn't just sex. It really was lovemaking.

T.J., fully clothed, her hair damp from a quickie shower was not surprised to see Angelo had remained despite her request that he leave.

"I suppose you think this means something. It doesn't you know. It just happened. I was angry and you, well you, you..."

Michael didn't give T.J. time to finish. He was kissing her again. This time, they undressed quicker than before. Once again, the thought flickered in T.J.'s mind that the door was unlocked and why in the hell didn't this man have a condom or something. But soon, like before, she was beyond caring about anything except the wonderful pleasure Angelo was giving her and by the sounds he was making, she was giving him.

When it was all over, T.J. didn't bother to move for the longest time. Later, they took turns using her bathroom and walked hand in hand down the stairs, past an angry looking Cora back to the pier.

"Angelo, I don't know what to say."

"Say you love me. Say what happened back there was as incredible for you as it was for me. Say you'll marry me."

"Angelo, I can't marry you."

"Why not, for Heaven's sake?"

"Because, I told you. I had a talk with Mr.Colarossi last night."

"But, if he told you who I really am, then why would you not want to marry me. I can't promise you a safe, routine life, but I do swear I'll love you forever and I will never let you go."

Visions of the Diane Keaton character trying to divorce young Michael Corleone and losing her kids in the bargain made T.J. shiver.

"That's why I could never marry you," she said sadly just as his beeper went off.

Michael looked at a number that had flashed on the side of the gadget, then pulled his tiny cellular out and dialed a number. He could only watch as T.J. headed back to the house.

He spoke curtly to the caller, then hurried to his rented car. He almost turned back to see if he could make things right with T.J., then decided it might be better to give her a little time to sort things out. He didn't doubt for a moment that she loved him as much as he loved her.

*   *   *

Steve lived in a small Acadian cottage on Bayou Teche. His place was warm and comfortable. He had furnished it with French antiques found in the shops along Magazine and Royal Streets in New Orleans.

T.J. was seated on a large over-stuffed sofa sipping a glass of wine and hugging a throw pillow with cherubs on it. When she realized one of the small angels looked just like Angelo, she tossed the pillow on the floor. A few seconds later, she picked it up again, studied the angel closely, then clasped the pillow to her breasts with an audible sigh.

"What's wrong?" Stephen was moving back and forth from the kitchen to the living room. He was making shrimp Creole and the wonderful aroma was making her stomach growl.

"Nothing. I'm starving. When do we eat?"

"Now," he said leading T.J. to his formal dining room. The table was set with his good china. Two crystal candleholders with cream-colored tapers leant a romantic air to the room.

The old friends chatted comfortably, catching up. T.J. had never talked to Steve about her recent troubles. She had shared everything with John and look what happened. She was even more confused now, but how could she tell the man she was going to marry that she had just lost her virginity and was still marveling at the magic of it.

After dinner, T.J. and Stephen cuddled on the sofa for a short time. He had not tried to kiss her. In fact, in anticipation of the formal proposal both were a little shy with each other. After a while, he got up and left the room briefly. He returned carrying a small velvet box and handed it to T.J.

The diamond was close to three karats and T.J. gasped when she saw it.

"Try it on," Steve laughed when he saw her expression.

"Wow. It's beautiful," T.J. whispered, slipping the ring on her finger. Then, she started sobbing. Loud, soul-wrenching sobs that alarmed Stephen.

"Does this mean yes or no?"

T.J. couldn't talk and Steve took her silence to mean she was crying because she was so happy. He embraced T.J. 'til the sobs lessened, then stopped. He kissed her gently, then started to undo her shirt. She glanced around wildly trying to figure out a way to halt his advances without angering him and causing him to call off the wedding. Steve was trying unsuccessfully to pull off her jeans. They weren't budging. They both started laughing.

"Don't tell me you see Sister?"

T.J. was about to answer when his phone rang and he went to the kitchen to answer it. T.J. was so glad to get the unexpected reprieve, she hurriedly buttoned her shirt and headed for the bathroom. They returned to the living room at the same time.

"I have an emergency at the hospital. Will you wait here for me 'til I get back?"

"How long will you be?"

"I don't know. This may take a while."

"I need to head back to the City really early tomorrow. But Steve, will you call me in the morning. I want to talk with you before I leave. OK?"

"Sure. In fact, I'll call when I get back tonight if it's not too late. I love you."

"I love you, too," T.J. said, and meaning it with all her heart. She just didn't think she knew what being in love was all about. She had certainly thought she was in love with John. She was very much in lust with Angelo. But in love with him? She definitely loved Stephen. Had loved him all her life in fact. She kissed him to reassure herself that she was doing the right thing, marrying him. The kiss was comfortable, nice. They fit. She would be happy spending the rest of her life with him.

So maybe she wasn't **in love** with Steve, and maybe she didn't feel the heat, the passion she had felt only a few hours earlier with Angelo. Still, she knew she had made the wisest choice.

"I do love you, Dr. Rose," she said vehemently before they parted for the evening.

Chapter 12

Dating Games II

T.J. was telling Lawanna about her weekend. The diamond engagement ring flashed as she waved her arms about, delighting her friend as she unraveled her latest escapades.

"So, thank God," she said, "he couldn't get my pants off, cause I had already done it once that day. Can you imagine having sex with two different men on the very day you lost your virginity? I mean, I kept thinking, God's gonna punish me for doing it before I get married. But maybe HE wouldn't be as upset if at least I had made love to the man I was going to marry. But then I felt even more guilty about almost doing it with Steve."

"But T.J., did you enjoy it?"

"It was the most wonderful thing. You know when I got back home, and was showing my ring to Mama and Daddy, Cora walked in. Cora kept staring at me. She knew. She had put clean sheets on my bed. She kept saying, she didn't understand why I just didn't marry that nice Dr. Rose and I realized she thought I was engaged to Angelo. So when Mama told her I **was** going to marry Dr. Rose, Cora looked at me for the first time in my life as if I was going straight to hell. But I didn't care."

"Enough about Cora, Girl. What happened when Steve called?"

"Nothing. I told him I loved him. We plan to see each other Saturday night to set the wedding date."

"Good Lord, T.J. Let me see if I got this straight. This weekend you were kidnapped by the grocery bag man and brought to an old Godfather. Lost your virginity, in fact, made passionate love twice to a Mafia loan shark, and then had the nerve to get engaged to your other best friend. I need chocolate."

"How about a glass of wine? What did you do?" T.J. asked reaching in the refrigerator for the Chablis.

"Nothing. Saved a couple of lives. Nothing. So what's going to happen now?"

"I go to work tomorrow as usual. Oh, I forgot to tell you. I didn't even think about gambling once. In fact, losing my pants to Angelo was a hell-of-a lot more fun than losing them to craps. Dear God, I've got to put him out of my mind." Out of my heart, she thought, but didn't add.

The phone sounded shrill and both women jumped, then laughed at their nervous reaction.

"John," T.J. took a deep breath and pleaded silently to Lawanna for help.

*   *   *

It was almost 7 p.m. and T.J., clad in new black pants and a really low-cut silk shirt hurried along Conti to the Royal Sonnesta Hotel at the corner of Bourbon. She entered the Mystic Den lounge glancing around nervously. John was already there and stood to greet her.

"Thank you for coming," he said solemnly. "We really need to talk."

"Yes, I know. But, John, I don't have much time. I'm meeting my fiancée' for dinner in a little while."

"Your fiancée'?"

"That's why I agreed to meet you here, I wanted to tell you in person."

"You're engaged." John stated the fact, but gave T.J. no indication how the news affected him.

"Look, John. You don't really love me. I don't know what happened between us on the boat, but I was so miserable and you were there for me. But, you..." T.J. stopped short as the bartender approached and asked to take their orders. John ordered Scotch on the rocks but T.J. just stared, then mumbled, "A glass of wine. White. Dry."

Michael, with his black hair lightened considerably and sporting a small gold hoop merely smiled at T.J. before moving off to fill their orders. He liked this disguise.

"Is something wrong? You look like you saw a ghost."

"No, It's just the bartender reminds me of someone I used to know." John leaned close to T.J. "About us," he started to say.

"There is no us. I'm engaged and now you're free to pursue that strange little hood who is sulking at the end of the bar pretending not to notice us."

"Jimmy? He's here?" John turned to look in the direction T.J. indicated just as Michael returned with their drinks.

"Excuse me. I'll take care of him," John said heading in Jimmy's direction.

"I need to talk with you," Michael said urgently.

"Angelo," T.J. said gulping her glass of wine, "I want another drink."

"T.J., what are you doing with him? I thought you were throwing me over for Steve Rose. Talk to me."

"No. Another glass of wine, please."

"OK, but don't go away."

John walked back and sat down next to T.J. "You know, T.J., I'm not denying who I am and what I am. The thing is I love you. I told Jimmy it's over between him and me. Again." John was whispering intensely in T.J.'s ear when Michael returned with her wine. He placed it in front of her without a word.

T.J. drank the whole glass of wine at once and turned to John.

"What do you want from me? Don't you think I'm confused enough anyway? You're all making me crazy. What am I going to do?"

"Huh? So you don't really want to marry...by the way, who are you going to marry?"

"Stephen Rose."

"You're going to marry Steve? I mean, I knew you were friends, but I thought that was it. You were just good friends."

"Well…" T.J. turned to make sure Angelo wasn't listening. She took a long sip of John's scotch.

"You want another drink? Bartender. Another glass of wine, please."

"No...aw shit," she said as she saw Angelo move to the back of the bar to prepare her drink.

"Look, I know your grandpa is gonna be upset. I think he really wanted me to marry into the family, if you know what I mean. But, like I told him, I'm going to marry Steve. I want to settle down, start my family."

Michael placed the glass of wine in front of T.J. and said quietly, "Can I talk with you, Miss? It's very important."

"I told you 'no'," T.J. answered sharply.

"You need to stop bothering my friend. Do I know you?"

"I don't think so," Michael said moving away before Conti remembered the clumsy fisherman with the hook in his head.

"Goodbye, John," T.J. said, looking at her watch. "I'm supposed to meet Steve in the lobby at 7:30 and I'm late."

T.J. gulped her wine, pecked John on the cheek and rushed out to the lobby with Michael in pursuit. She collided with Steve who had his back to her and put her arms around him to brace herself. Michael ran into her and grabbed her around the waist to prevent a fall. "Sorry, Miss," he said as his hands crept up to grope her boobs. Sandwiched between the two of them, and responding to Angelo's bold sexual touch, she decided she really needed another drink. Fast. She pushed

Angelo off of her and practically shoved Steve across the hall to the entrance of the Begues restaurant.

T.J. was drinking another glass of wine and was starting to feel a little giddy. She was trying to listen as Steve talked about their engagement and upcoming marriage. But all she could think about was Angelo. She wanted so much to feel his hands on her body again. She felt herself blushing as she thought about making love to him in her bedroom.

"Are you all right? You seem a little flushed."

"Oh, I'm fine. It's just a little warm in here," T.J. responded as the waiter approached to take their orders.

Steve ordered the medallion of veal and T.J. decided to try the restaurant's variation of shrimp Creole. The waiter had not spoken and when he asked what sort of dressings they wanted on their salads, T.J. looked up and smiled. "Oil and vinegar," she said. "Uh, could I talk with you?"

"Now?"

"Yes, now." T.J. drained her glass and stood up, somewhat shakily. "Steve, I'll be right back. I need to talk with uh-our waiter."

Steve stared at the two of them, and not knowing what to make of the situation, merely nodded in assent as T.J. grabbed the waiter by the arm and dragged him out of the restaurant.

"Do you have a room here?"

"I can get one. Wait here."

Five minutes later, T.J. was tearing Angelo's clothes off.

"I can't believe this. Hurry."

"I'm hurrying," Michael said, jumping under the covers."

Their bodies were so starved for each other, they couldn't stop making love. One climax after another until a somewhat sober T.J. said she needed to get back to Steve.

As she headed for the door leaving Michael exhausted on the king-sized bed, she said. "It's just sex, you know. I have to make up for twenty-seven years without it. It's just sex."

"Sure," Michael responded. "Great sex." Then he laughed.

When T.J. got back to the table, a near-starved Steve was trying to find out what happened to their order. He poured a couple of drops from an empty wine bottle and was berating a young waitress who was in tears. He took one look at T.J. and told her that he had a thermometer in his bag in the car and was going to go get it.

"I'm fine," she insisted. "Let's get out of here. Go back to my place. I just need some air."

T.J. and Steve, arms entwined supported each other as they stumbled back to her apartment. T.J. had sobered enough to know she was in big trouble. She wasn't being fair to Steve, carrying on with Angelo like some sort of nympho, but she couldn't help herself. All she could think about was being with him. She blushed with pleasure just thinking about him and his perfect body. She had made love with him once again without contraception. What if she got pregnant? She could never marry him. Never. She was not cut out to be married to the Mob. She looked up at Steve as they entered her apartment. She had never seen her friend this drunk before. She knew what she had to do.

*   *   *

T.J. walked back into the bedroom where Steve was just beginning to stir. She wore an oversized tee with nothing underneath.

"Good morning, sleepyhead," she practically chirped to her puzzled-looking fiancée.

Steve glanced at the chair with his sport coat and slacks draped neatly across and peered under the covers to confirmed what he feared. Totally naked.

"What happened?"

"You don't remember? How could you not remember?" T.J. pretended to be majorly disappointed.

"The last thing I remember is coming through that door and your breaking out that bottle of champagne to celebrate our engagement. Don't tell me you finally saw Sister and I don't even remember. Oh, T.J., I'm so sorry."

"I forgive you."

"Well, come over here and let me find out what I missed."

At the moment Steve's beeper blared and he groaned as he reached for the phone next to the bed. "Not again."

"Looks like you'll have to take my word for it. It was wonderful," T.J. pouted as Steve took the cordless phone into the bathroom, then came out, dressed hurriedly and kissed T.J. very seriously before leaving.

T.J. felt more and more guilty as she thought about what she'd done. How could she lie to Steve like that? How could she not? She was going to marry the man. If she was lucky enough not to let her moments of craziness with Angelo leave her pregnant, font thank God. But, if she was, well then, Steve would make a wonderful father and husband. She thought about getting pregnant. She had friends who'd tried unsuccessfully for years to become pregnant. But on the other hand she had friends who had had abortions because they got caught the first time they did it. Please God, she thought, don't let me be pregnant.

Chapter 13

T.J.'s Little Problem II

T.J. wiped the sweat from her brow with a cold, damp towel that she carried from the bathroom. Although it was the middle of one of the hottest Junes in New Orleans history, the window unit was keeping the apartment fairly cool. In fact, Lawana was draped in one of Grandma Connie's creations.

"Well, are you gonna keep me in suspense," the young doctor asked.

"It turned blue," T.J. said applying the cloth to her forehead as she plopped next to her friend.

"Wow, I'm gonna be an Auntee," Lawana yelled, throwing her arms around T.J. who pushed her away before racing to the bathroom to throw up for the third time that morning.

When T.J. returned to the living room with a fresh wash cloth and an embarrassed grin, she hugged her friend.

"I'm going to be a mother. Me. A mother. Can you believe it?" Before Lawana could answer. "I'm too young to be a mother. What do I know about babies? Nothing. I know nothing about children. I'm not even married. I need to be a wife for a while before I can be a mother. Don't you think?" And before her friend could respond. "At least I'm a fiancée. But I'm not engaged to my baby's father. How can I marry someone who will only think he's the father, when the real

father won't even know he's the father. Well, you're awfully quiet.
Don't you have anything to say about the most momentous thing
that's ever happened to me?"

"Yeah. I have one thing to say. I thank God every day, I have you for
a friend. Or else, my life would be like riding the kiddie train in
Audubon Park instead of taking one gigantic roller-coaster ride."

"Which reminds me," T.J. said as she ran off to the bathroom again,
leaving her friend laughing joyfully at the newest episode in T.J.
Marino's hilarious saga.

      *   *   *

T.J. wondered what she was going tell her parents. Actually she
couldn't even decide if she should say anything at all right away. She
wouldn't be showing for a few months. Far more pressing at the
moment was what she was going to say to Steve.

She glanced at the clock on the dashboard as she drove more cautiously than usual toward Tallula. Almost 2 p.m. Sharing her secret
with Lawana this morning had helped. Although her friend couldn't
tell her what to do, she knew Lawanna would be there for her whatever
she decided.

She just couldn't predict how Mamma and Daddy were going to take
the news. They were so happy about her engagement. About the possibility of having her back in Tallula again. And, if she were presenting
them with their first grandchild after the wedding instead of before,
they would be ecstatic.

But living in a small town, people would talk, even if it was the 21st
century and half the young women in Tallula were single mothers. In
fact, one friend of T.J.'s, a couple of years younger, even had triplets.
There was the usual gossip at first, most of it fueled by Emelda Walters.
Then everyone rallied to help the young mother and she was doing
quite well.

It was very hot and humid and the car's air-conditioner was barely keeping the Honda cool. T.J. was looking forward to relaxing by the pool, a tall glass of iced tea and maybe a piece of Cora's blackberry pie. She was starving and as she switched on the car radio to the cheery banter of WWL's disc jockeys, she tried to imagine what it was going to be like to become a mother. Although the idea was new and scary, T.J. smiled to herself.

"You must have been a beautiful baby, cause baby look at you now," T.J. sang, remembering how wonderful making this child with Angelo had been. She blushed just thinking about it.

But as she turned into her parent's drive, a frown replaced the smile and she took three very deep breaths as her mama raced out to greet her.

*   *   *

"Mama," T.J. said, then rushed past Diana who had extended her arms for the usual embrace.

"Cora," T.J. said, brushing past the astounded housekeeper and into the nearest guest bath.

Diana and Cora stood outside the locked bathroom door listening as T.J. loudly emptied her stomach.

"Cora, you don't think she has bulimia, do you?" Diana whispered, mortified at the thought.

"Now, Miz Marino, you know that girl ain't got no bulimia, whatever that is. And the good Lord will strike me dead for thinking what I'm thinking."

"What are you thinking?" Cora just gave her the look that meant, "Don't kid yourself, you know what I'm thinking, cause you're thinking the same thing."

"No," Diana said as T.J. emerged, a damp gold-trimmed guest towel held to her lips.

"T.J., you aren't..." Diana couldn't continue.

"Going to hell," Cora finished.

"Not at all. I'm just pregnant," T.J. smiled grimly leaving the two women speechless as she bounded up the stairs with her trusty duffel.

       *   *   *

The Marinos ate in silence and even Cora was unusually quiet as she cleared away plates of barely touched etouffee.

"I don't suppose you and Steve could have waited?" Diana asked as Cora placed large servings of warm blackberry cobbler topped with vanilla ice cream in front of them.

The three of them waited for T.J.'s response.

"I can't talk about this now, OK?" T.J. pleaded.

"OK, but does Steve know?"

T.J. was looking at Cora, very sure she made the connection between Angelo's visit to her bedroom and her present condition. She smiled as she remembered the incredible time they had had making this baby. Diana's question didn't really register.

"I hope not," T.J. replied to the bewilderment of her parents.

"Then, when do you plan to tell him, before or after the wedding?" Diana asked sarcastically.

"Di," Tony began.

"Don't Di me. Don't you dare. You men are all alike. You just want one thing. And you don't care who you hurt."

T.J. looked at both her parents. She hadn't realized they were still fighting about his indiscretion with his secretary. T.J. was worried about them. They had never gone this long without forgiving each other. T.J. couldn't imagine either one of them living without the other.

Diana wiped perspiration off her brow and dipped into her iced tea for a cube to rub on her cheeks. She excused herself and ran from the room, ranting about the damn humidity.

Tony, who under normal circumstances would have followed her, merely walked to the sideboard and poured himself a scotch and water. He returned to the table and nervously confronted his daughter.

"T.J., we do need to talk."

"Yes, child, we need to talk," Cora came in and sat down in the chair Diana had vacated.

"I'm pregnant. I'm going to be a mother. I'm going to marry Steve Rose. I don't know when. Well, I do know when I'm having the baby. Around the 15th of February. Daddy, you've always wanted to be a Paw Paw. So, be happy and help me with Mama. OK?"

Tony rose and took T.J. in his arms.

Cora muttered "humph," but was tearful as she picked up the dessert dishes and left the table.

*   *   *

T.J. and Steve were lounging on brightly striped beach towels on the pool deck. Steve had attended a conference in Dallas on Saturday, and now they were enjoying a lazy, uninterrupted Sunday afternoon. Doc Romero was on call and even Cora was cooperating by leaving them alone. Tony and Diana had stepped out earlier to say Hello-Goodbye, then left hand in hand to go see a matinee at the old Arcade Theater in Morgan City.

"So, alone at last. I know you said you don't want to make love again until after we're married, but if you want to go inside so we can do it with me awake and sober, I really wouldn't mind."

"Steve, there's something I need to tell you."

"You sound so serious. Is something wrong?"

"I'm pregnant."

"Pregnant? Are you sure? I mean, that's wonderful. Do you want to get married now?"

"That's just it. I don't know if I want to get married at all."

"You don't? T.J., that doesn't make sense. I thought you loved me. Having our baby just makes me that more determined to make you my wife."

"You don't understand. This baby…" T.J. looked at Steve and realized that she could not hurt him, "this baby will be due in February. Maybe we could get married in the spring. Like in April or something."

"After the baby is born? Why?"

"Because that way I'll know you're not marrying me just because I'm pregnant."

"T.J., we decided to get married before you got pregnant."

"Oh, all right. In April."

T.J. realized Steve was giving in without a real fight because he wanted them to be married and was not going to do anything to jeopardize their chances. She felt a little better having told him about the baby. Not much, but a little.

     *   *   *

"So we set a tentative date for around the middle of April."

Lawanna sat quietly without commenting as T.J. went on and on about the weekend.

"What?"

"I didn't say anything."

"That's the problem. So, what's wrong?"

"We're best friends, aren't we?"

"Of course we are."

"Then how come you haven't asked me to be the Godmother?"

"So that's what's bothering you." T.J. laughed. "You can be the Godmother."

"Great. Now does that mean if she's a girl you're gonna name her after me?"

"Lawanna? Guess again. No way I'm going to name a white girl Lawanna. Now maybe if it's a boy."

The two young woman talked for hours Sunday night. T.J. told her friend about her parent's reconciliation and support for her pregnancy. Although Diana was not happy about T.J.'s decision to marry until after the baby was born, she figured her sisters would approve because their niece was marrying the child's father and a doctor at that.

Tony promised to throw the biggest wedding the people of Tallula ever saw. He was the Mayor after all. Even Cora seemed relieved that T.J. was going to settle down, and by the time T.J. left, had stopped asking God to forgive "this poor little lamb who just lost her way."

Every once in a while, T.J. would run to the bathroom, then return to the living room with a Sprite soda or ginger cookie or whatever she could find to stop the nausea. Lawanna left about 1:15a.m. She had had a rare weekend off and was scheduled to be at the hospital in just a few hours.

T.J. kissed her friend on the cheek as they said goodnight, then went to bed without her usual long soak in bubbles. She was getting a new case in the morning and she wanted to be fresh and focused, if at all possible.

That night T.J. dreamed she was pushing three baby boys in a huge carriage. A nice little ole lady who looked like Angelo in drag stopped to admire the tots. "Oh, how cute," she cooed as she lifted the hood of the carriage. Smiling up at her were three tiny babies with adult faces. They all looked like Angelo. And they were all black. "What are their names?" the old lady asked. "I call them La, Wan, and Na," T.J. answered. The dream did not waken T.J. She smiled in her sleep.

Chapter 14

Oh, Oh, Angelo

The meeting place on Rigolets smelled musty. It was late August and had rained for several days. The mood in the shut-down restaurant matched the heavy darkness outside.

Frankie Modella stood up and faced the young Don.

"Boss, we got the scoop on that DeLuca character."

"OK, shoot."

"You sure you want to hear this?"

"Frankie, don't waste my time."

"Anything you say, Boss, but you aren't going to like it."

"Frankie." The name was spoken softly, but the young man's eyes were as deadly as black ice.

"He's Feds."

"He's what?"

"I told you you didn't want to hear it."

"Well, I heard it. OK, how much does he know?"

"I don't know."

"What's his real name."

"I don't know."

"Does anybody here know anything?"

The men were seated at a dilapidated round table covered in a yellow-ing cloth. Frankie Modella turned to look at Joseph Romano who looked at Johnnie Sabatori who looked at Phil Sacco who looked at the Don.

"I guess we don't know nuthing," Frankie ventured bravely.

"You want me to ice him, Boss?" Joseph Romano, alias Joey the Jackal had been the best hammer in the heydays of Marcello's reign as Louisiana Mafia boss. As he approached his ninetieth birthday, Joey's offer to kill Angelo might seem ludicrous to an outsider. But no one in the room laughed because Joey was still used on occasion, particularly since he carried with him the much-needed element of surprise. Who would dream the decrepit old man who could barely move was so dangerous?

"I'll handle this one, Joey. Thanks."

The group sat for an hour or so doing business. Mostly trying to fig-ure out how to set up a new slot distributorship for a couple of casinos slated to open in the Shreveport area in a few years.

After the others left, the young Don poured himself another glass of wine and thought about Angelo Deluca. Except for the tight-knit little group of loyal followers he had just met with, no one knew of his con-nection to Frankie Colarossi. So, in a sense, Deluca didn't really pose a threat. Still the Don's antenna was up. Despite the ancient Mafia code that killing cops was strictly off limits, something was going to have to be done to take Deluca out of the picture. He wasn't sure just what, but it was time he paid another visit to his Godfather. He wanted to talk with him about T.J. again anyway.

T.J. More and more he realized how much she meant to him. He wanted to spend every day of his life with her. He knew that T.J. loved him. The rest would happen. The one thing he'd learned from the Family was patience. He could wait.

*   *   *

The young Don, who made it a point to seldom visit his Godfather at his home found himself entering the premises again through a hidden basement door that only he used. None of Frankie's bodyguards seemed to be around.

Frankie was laying on a daybed in the glassed-in sunroom at the back of the house facing the river. Vinyl venetian blinds were closed tightly, and the old man appeared to be asleep."

"**Parran**," the young Don coaxed. Wake up?"

"What? Oh, it's you. What time is it?"

"It's late. I shouldn't have come, but I need your help."

The young man told his Godfather what he had learned about Angelo Deluca and Frankie listened without interrupting as was his habit.

"The thing is, I don't think he'll go away without a little push."

"You know how I feel about offing law enforcement."

"I know. That's why I came to you for advice."

The young Don and his mentor discussed ways to dispose of Angelo Deluca and finally came up with a solution that they both could live with.

"I'll put Joey on it right away, but now I need to tell you about T.J."

"I already heard."

"You have? Who...never mind. What do you think?"

"Who cares what an old man thinks? Does Johnnie know?"

The young Don didn't want to say anything about Conti that would anger Frankie who was fond of his grandson.

"What does Johnnie care?" he asked perturbed.

"I did'n know," Frankie shrugged.

*   *   *

A week later, Michael Zello was sitting in a waterfront condo about a mile from the Mafia's secret meeting place on Rigolets Road. He was reporting to fifty-year-old Mark O'Keefe the supervisor of Operation Naughty games. The older man didn't like what he was hearing.

"Listen Mike," he said. "Are you telling me that John Conti is not the man we're after?"

"No, Mark," I'm telling you I don't know. All I know for sure about Conti is he's Colarossi's grandson and he's gay."

"OK. Let me get this straight, Mike. The guy you've been tailing all this time is a gay Italian who may or may not be the most powerful man in the Louisiana Mob. Come on."

"Well, who else?"

"I don't know. Find out. That's your job, Mike. What about the Marino woman? Has she been cooperative?"

"Very", Michael found himself blushing just thinking about how cooperative T.J. had been. "She's shared what she can and I am incredibly appreciative of her contribution."

"So, what's your plan?"

"The other day, I found I was being followed by this old fellow and..."

"Old, how old?"

"Real old, like 100?"

"How could he be following you? In a wheelchair?"

"No, I'm sure it was some sort of disguise. The shuffle, the cane. All an act. So, anyway, I confronted him."

"What did you do, wave a feather in his face?"

"Not funny. I just eased him over in front of Maison Blanche on Canal Street the other day and asked him why he was following me."

"And he said I reminded him of his long lost great-grandson who disappeared when he was about my age. The old fellow said rumor had it that the young man had been hooked up with the Mob and swimming with the fishes at the bottom of Lake Ponchartrain."

"You believe him?"

"Pretty strange. I'm checking him out. I'll let you know. I'd better be going. I'll see you back here next week."

"Yeah. Oh, by the way, Mike, see if you can come up with big, bad-wiseguy-suspects a little more believable than a queen and a centenarian."

"You know your problem, Mark, is you have no imagination. And that fact is going to get you killed someday. These two people are dangerous. Sheep's clothing dangerous. And, some of us are more cautious than others because we can sense the disguise. Others can't."

"Sure, sure. Michael Zello, master of disguise. Get the hell out of here, Mr. Angelo Deluca and don't forget to watch your back."

O'Keefe was still laughing as Michael left the stilt-supported condo.

    *   *   *

The young Don looked at the large glossy photos of Angelo Deluca and Joey Romano. Perfect, he thought. The Feds are so stupid, they'll never know what's going on 'til it's too late. Angelo Deluca was a goner. He put the pictures in a large manila envelope and smiled.

Chapter 15
Thanks Be

The trip to Tallula was taking much too long. T.J couldn't get comfortable behind the steering wheel. Her stomach took up too much room. The seat was pushed back as far as possible to accommodate T.J.'s almost overnight expansion, so her legs could barely reach the gas pedal. She kept adjusting the small soft pillow at the small of her back, but that wasn't helping much.

Thanksgiving. T.J. loved the Turkey Holiday almost as much as Christmas. The whole clan went to Aunt Frances' for dinner. She lived in a beautiful old home on Main Street in Franklin, a short fifteen minutes from Tallula.

The house was too big for one person, but Uncle Johnny had left her Aunt well-off. So despite periodic heavy losses at the casinos, Frances could afford the hired help that it took to maintain the home and its lush gardens. She had several retirement accounts that she wouldn't need to touch 'til she turned fifty-nine, still several years away.

Frances and the other two Sisters had accepted T.J.'s pregnancy better than anyone had anticipated. They had already started buying small gifts for the baby and Frances had opened a really generous trust fund for her grandniece. She was sure it was going to be a girl, despite T.J.'s opposition to finding out the sex beforehand.

T.J. was getting more and more excited about being a mother. She had arranged for three months paid leave from the office and another month of vacation time if needed when the baby was born.

One of the advantages of working for an all-female law firm was a no-guilt attitude about having babies and a career at the same time. The baby could even come to work with her if she chose.

Now that she wasn't throwing up all the time, she actually felt good. Things were starting to get better in general. With the help of a Gamblers Anonymous that met weekly in the Quarter, she'd even managed to stay away from the casinos.

Even her love life was becoming, if not ideal, at least saner. It had helped that she hadn't heard from John Conti since that night in the Mystic Den Lounge in New Orleans. Mama had heard that he'd gone back to the East Coast to help his mother care for his ailing father. Then, after John's father passed away, he'd stayed on with his mother at the family's country estate in New Jersey to help her settle her affairs. T.J. was glad he was away.

She was not so happy that Angelo was also out of her life. T.J. had refused to return his calls at first, even though she thought about him constantly and wanted more than anything to share this pregnancy with him. But when she thought about the child, she knew she didn't want this precious gift to end up like Michael Corleone. He, too, was an innocent who ended up a killer and head of the Mafia. Her son was never going to know about his Mafia father if she could help it. Anyway, she had called Angelo and pleaded with him to leave her alone. Completely alone for six months. Then, she told him, they would have a serious conversation about their relationship.

Michael had reluctantly agreed not to call her, not to follow her. To pretend she never existed and he didn't think about her all the time and just wanted to make love to her every moment of every day.

T.J. almost gave in when he said those things to her over the phone. But she hadn't.

T.J.'s attention was brought back to the present when she realized her favorite song from a few years back was being played by WWL. Whitney Houston. "I will always love you." Tears fell as T.J. thought of Angelo and how easily he had given in to her foolish request. "I wish you love and I will always love you," T.J. sang along with Whitney. She missed Angelo so much. "Where are you?" she asked out loud after the song had ended. T.J. looked at the clock on the dashboard. Almost there.

Steve, unlike Angelo, hadn't been so agreeable about her wishes and T.J.'s thoughts drifted to him and his constant pleas that they marry. Especially, as she started showing.

But, as the baby grew, so did her love for Angelo and she absolutely refused to set a definite date for the wedding. Steve wasn't going to be pacified much longer and it was almost time for her to face Angelo.

As she pulled into the drive at Fair Oaks, T.J. felt safe. Lately, her parents had been making her feel that way. Protected. She knew that she and her baby would always have a safe haven in her parents' bayou home.

*   *   *

Aunt Frances had the mahogany dining room table beautifully set for her twelve guests. She was decked out in a gold velvet leopard jumpsuit. Her hair was short, the red altered to a Rodman blonde for the occasion. She looked younger than her sisters. She'd been under the cosmetic surgeon's knife several times. Everything from face lifts to boob enhancements to liposuction.

Frances hugged and kissed T.J. She patted Tony on the back and smiled at Cora after her young white-aproned maid had ushered them all in.

Cora handed her coat to the maid and made herself at home in the dark plum living room. Cora was always relieved of her housekeeping duties on Thanksgiving and she loved being waited on this one day of the year. The food was catered and wasn't as good as what she herself prepared, but that didn't matter. She was a guest today. A member of the family everyday and a guest today.

One by one the other invited guests arrived. T.J. was seated next to Cora on a bright orange slip-cover style sofa. They remained side by side in an unlikely receiving line as the others came in to say hello and see how big T.J.'d gotten.

"Hello, T.J., Cora," Aunt Annie said. "Look how good you look. Praise the Lord."

"Praise the Lord," Cora agreed.

"Thank you, Aunt Annie. Is Uncle Carlo coming?"

"Sure, he'll be here. He doesn't miss a day of hunting you know. He's just running a little late, but he'll be able to smell that turkey as soon as it's on the table. Let me go see if I can help your mama and Aunt Frances supervise. See you in a little while."

Cora turned to T.J. "I heard after she joined that space ship church, your Uncle Carlo just up and left her. Moved in with one of his bimbos."

"Get out of here." Cora started to leave. "No, Cora, stay. I mean, Mama didn't say anything."

"Well, it's all hush-hush. Here comes the other sister."

"Aunt Lucie, Uncle James," T.J. rose to hug the couple.

"You're huge, T.J."

"Huge," Uncle James repeated.

"Well, I've put on a few pounds since last month."

"But how are you feeling? You look good. Don't you think so, Cora?"

"Cora?" Uncle James echoed.

Cora just looked at the two of them like they were nuts and T.J. answered. "I feel good."

"That's good. We need to go help Frances, James," Lucie said escorting her husband to the kitchen.

"There must be twenty hired hands in the kitchen. I don't think your Auntie needs any more help, do you?"

"Oh, you know, Cora. They're just a little uncomfortable with me being pregnant, you know, unmarried and all." Like it didn't matter to Cora.

"Speaking of married, here's Steve and his mama."

Steve had his arm around his mother as they entered the living room. Claire Rose had not aged well. She had deep wrinkles from years of smoking. She was proud of her physician son, but no amount of free medical advice and admonition from him could get Claire to give up the habit. Claire had always been pretty much a loner and often cigarettes were her only companion.

Claire didn't know what to make of the situation between T.J. and Steve. She had practically raised this girl who had spent so much time with her son growing up, but she didn't understand her. Didn't really understand Steve either. Young people today. Still she was happy about being a grandmother soon. She hugged T.J. tightly.

Recoiling slightly from the strong cigarette smell, T.J. turned to Steve and gave him a sweet peck on the cheek. He was offended by the gesture and kissed her fully on the lips. Cora, who had been observing the scenario with her usual curiosity, grunted a prayer.

Frances appeared from nowhere to announce brunch was being served. It was almost 2 p.m., too late for lunch and too early for supper. So, as usual, it was Thanksgiving brunch.

As T.J. entered the hunter green dining room and took her seat next to Steve, she noticed two chairs were unoccupied. She realized that Uncle Carlo had not yet arrived and Aunt Annie was fanning herself and trying to ignore the empty seat next to her. The other vacant place was to the left of Aunt Frances who sat at the head of the table.

"Who wants to say the blessing? T.J.?"

"Please. Why don't we wait for Father Hebert," T.J. said, assuming that the empty chair next to Aunt Frances was for him.

"Uh, Henry's not going to be with us today. He's spending Thanksgiving with his sister who's in Oschners with pneumonia."

"I'll say it," Tony offered to the groans of everyone at the table who was hungry and knew how wordy Tony could be.

"Thank you, Lord for bringing us all together. For our health. For the baby, our grandchild, that's growing inside of our daughter. For the love that she and Steve share. Especially for…"

"Praise the Lord," Cora cut him off.

"Amen," Annie finished.

Just around the time a uniformed butler brought the golden turkey surrounded by cornbread dressing in on a huge platter, the doorbell rang. Shortly after, Annie's very tipsy husband staggered in. His shirt-tail was hanging out, hair uncombed and his pants were unzipped.

"How was the hunting, darling?" Annie asked, her voice as sharp as the carving knife on the side of the sterling turkey platter.

Everyone turned and watched as Carlo, without missing a beat answered, "I got my deer, dear." Then they all looked away.

Conversation was loud and happy during the meal when the doorbell rang again. This time a young man of about thirty with a ponytail and gold studs entered the room. He apologized for being late, then sat next to Frances. He put his arm possessively around her during introductions. Tim Boudreaux seemed very much at home. The Sisters looked him up and down, then questioned Frances with their eyes. Frances ignored them. She did, however, have the decency to turn beet red.

T.J. looked around the table. Her family. She loved the people here today. Warts and all. She was happy and hungry. She had double helpings of turkey and honey-baked ham, cornbread and rice stuffings, green bean casserole, sweet potatoes with marshmallows and pecans. Steve was charming and attentive to T.J. and this didn't go unnoticed by The Sisters who nodded their approval.

T.J. was really enjoying herself. Only one thing would have made it perfect. Having Angelo to share it all with. She hoped and prayed that he was having as special a day as she was. She wondered where he was as she served herself a third helping of cornbread dressing.

*   *   *

Michael Zello looked around the small cell. He took a hefty bite out of his Popeyes chicken leg and followed it with a tiny plastic fork-full of dirty rice. Not so bad, he thought.

He'd had worse Thanksgivings. Like the one he spent masquerading as a homeless person on the streets of Manhattan. He was tailing one of the under-bosses in an old Mafia clan when he was still a rookie with the Bureau. Several members of the Family were dining at Carmines having a delicious Thanksgiving affair, while he nibbled on a rubbery hot dog from a not-too-clean looking street vendor.

Yeah, this little hole in the wall jail in a no-name Louisiana hick town eating Popeye's was a hell of a lot better than being on the streets. He still hadn't figured out how he'd landed here.

He had been driving the two-laned back road that paralleled Highway 90 on his way from New Orleans to Lake Charles when stopped by a black and white not too far from Lafayette. Then arrested for supposedly going sixty-five in a fifty-five miles an hour zone. Not ticketed. Arrested.

And since he was incognito, he wasn't carrying his FBI ID. He didn't want to break his cover and believed he would be able to get out of jail as soon as he had a hearing. A hearing. That was a joke.

He'd been here two weeks. Wherever here was. He didn't know where he was, but something weird was going on. He was not allowed any phone calls, personal or otherwise. He had not been fingerprinted, but he had been stripped search.

His FBI issue firearm had been confiscated, leaving him feeling naked. Which was better than being handed the final insult, a faded orange jumpsuit that looked and smelled like it hadn't been washed since the last unlucky bastard who had worn it in this God-forsaken place.

He was the only prisoner in a two-cell lockup. But he was watched constantly by a couple of burly giants who didn't talk, not even to each other. They grunted in response to his questions. He had been trying to devise a plan to break out-he was FBI after all—but so far no brilliant ideas came to him.

Surely, O'Keefe would start looking for him. But it wasn't unusual for him to miss his weekly meetings with his supervisor. It could be weeks before a search was begun.

Michael was given back-issues of People Magazine and he was now familiar with all the happenings of the stars. He read all about the beautiful people of '97 in the issue where Tom Cruise graced its cover. Now old Tom would know how to get out of this situation. No impossible mission for him.

Mostly Michael thought about T.J. He should never have agreed to leave her alone. He needed her. Not just wanted her. He needed her like the old cliche, to breathe. He could barely function without her.

He was no further along in his quest to shut down Mafia operations in Louisiana and would make no progress until he identified and arrested the Mob's leader. He was spending too much time worrying about T.J. and how to win her over. He had resisted the impulse to see her despite his vow not to and he regretted that. Because now that their six month separation was almost over, he was locked away in a run-down town that probably not a soul knew existed except for the robot-like trooper who had arrested him and the two idiot guards.

He certainly hadn't seen anyone else in the town if it could be called that. He had arrived at night and the three or four dilapidated buildings on either side of the jail were dark. For all he knew they may have been abandoned years ago. Since he was fed only Popeyes and McDonalds, he didn't imagine the jail hired local people to cook or clean. Especially clean. The place was filthy as hell with roaches as big as his foot running around. When and if he got out, these people were going to pay big time.

Especially if T.J. was looking for him to tell him she had thought it over and missed him terribly and wanted to marry him instead of Steve Rose. Or worse, if she had given up on him and was already married to the damn doctor.

Michael needed to find a way out. He looked at the picture of Tom for the hundredth time. "Come on, Tommy boy, how would you get out of this mess?" Tom just smiled his sexy smile.

*   *   *

A week after Thanksgiving two things happened that affected the fate of Michael Zello, alias Angelo Deluca, and most recently, jailbird. First, T.J. had searched frantically for Angelo without luck. Heartbroken, she determined that maybe it was for the best. He'd obviously had had a change of heart or else he would have contacted her by now. She'd finally put it in the hands of St. Jude. She'd made a novena to the Saint of hopeless causes, and asked him to help her accept whatever happened.

She didn't suppose St. Jude thought it was a good idea for her to marry a Mafia man even if he was the father of her child. Now her only decision was whether or not she should marry Steve who still believed the baby was his. And rather than deceive her dear friend even more, she decided to tell him the truth and raise the child alone.

Around the same time, the young Don reported to Frankie Colarossi that the "Angelo Deluca thing" had been taken care of. The letter with the photo showing Angelo hobnobbing with a well-known Mafia killer had been sent to a special task force, unknown to the FBI, that investigated crime in Louisiana. The leader of the group was a popular politician and an old friend of Frankie Colarossi. Along with the photo was a memo stating that Joseph Romano had been arrested in New Orleans and had given a written confession that was attached to the memo.

Joey had described to the police how he and Deluca had plotted and carried out the demise of a local police officer who was on to one of their scams. The off-duty police officer had, indeed, died when his Camaro had smashed into a tree on River Road. The NOPD liked Joey's version a whole lot better than the truth. The officer was totally drunk at the time.

The task force decided, with Frankie's subtle input, that the matter would be handled locally and arrangements were made to have Deluca arrested by the State Police, but instead of turning him over to the local authorities in New Orleans, he would be transferred directly to the little abandoned town a few miles away from where he was picked up. The deserted jail had obviously been used before by both the Mob and unscrupulous law enforcement officers alike.

The legal-appearing abduction of Angelo Deluca was the coup of all time with too little paper work to trace the incident. Angelo would remain lost forever in that little ghost town. He would rot in the place.

The two Dons enjoyed a good laugh and a glass of wine together as they toasted Louisiana politics.

"Is Joey out of jail?" Frankie asked.

"Yeah," the young Don laughed. "They're not going to press charges against the old man. As long as he testifies against Deluca. If they ever find him."

Frankie raised his glass again. "To **ergastolo**."

To life in prison, the young Don thought as he toasted and laughed.

Chapter 16

Ho Ho Ho

T.J. and Lawanna dropped their packages on the floor and plopped on the sofa in T.J.'s apartment. Actually, T.J. sank, exhausted.

They had spent the afternoon at Maison Blanche on Canal doing last minute Christmas shopping. They both loved the holiday, but since the crowds at the malls seemed to get larger every year, they decided to try the neighborhood department store. Mr. Bingle had appeared in the store's window display every Christmas for as long as they could remember and they never tired of him.

The crowd, however, had been just as bad as the one at the malls. T.J. put her swollen feet up on the antique trunk that served as a coffee table.

"Well, Doc, what do you think? Am I going to make it another two months?"

Lawanna looked at her friend. She didn't like this quiet, depressed T.J.

"You're going to have to forget him, you know. He's gone. Out of the picture. You need to start making some plans for that baby who looks like it's about to pop out of you any day now."

"Don't you think I've tried?" T.J. regretted her angry tone immediately. "I'm sorry. It's not your fault Angelo's disappeared from the face of the earth. But I have a feeling something's wrong. He loves me, you know. He would not give up on me this easily. Something's wrong."

"What's wrong is the man's probably fallen for someone else. Seven months is a long time, Girl. Listen to me."

"Let's talk about something else, OK?"

The two friends spent a couple of hours chatting comfortably about nothing in particular, then exchanged fun gifts. T.J. gave Lawanna a huge chocolate moose and Lawanna gave T.J. a pair of fuzzy moose slippers to wear when her feet were too swollen to wear shoes. Shortly after, Lawanna left and T.J. packed for her Christmas vacation in Tallula.

*   *   *

T.J. awakened early on Christmas morning. Just like when she was a child. The house smelled like Christmas. Cedar tree, pine cones, oak firewood. The Christmas woods that blended into an aroma T.J. loved.

T.J. and Steve and her parents had made the rounds of open houses on Christmas Eve. They were offered everything from the traditional eggnog at the Walters' home to baked Italian sausage on French bread and potato salad at Aunt Annie's. T.J. had been surprised to find Uncle Carlo home until she heard Aunt Annie whisper something about him feeling a little under the weather. He looked as disheveled as he had at Thanksgiving. He was really getting too old for all the running around he did.

Anyway, everyone had had a wonderful time and Steve said he had a special surprise for her today. She couldn't imagine what it was.

Cora must have put the turkey in early this morning because already the delicious smell wafted upstairs to her room. Her bedside clock showed 7:30 a.m. and excited as a child expecting Santa Claus, T.J. slipped on her maternity coveralls and supporting her huge stomach, bounded down the stairs.

The tree in the Rose room was beautiful. It almost reached the tall ceiling and was decorated this year with angels. Gold angels and silver angels. Tiny ceramic cherubs and delicate crystal angels. Instead of a star, a large velvet-clad angel was perched on top, guarding all the lesser angels. The tree was lit by small, clear bulbs that enhanced rather than detracted from the heavenly theme.

T.J. ran to the kitchen and wished Cora a merry Christmas, grabbed a cup of decaf coffee and a biscuit and ran back to the living room to admire the tree with all the brightly wrapped gifts around it. She thought how wonderful it would be next year when her baby would celebrate its first Christmas. He or she would be almost a year old. And not fatherless, she decided.

Lawanna was right. She needed to get on with her life and do what's best for her baby. As she waited for Tony and Diana to join her to open presents, she determined that she would give Steve a definite date for the wedding. She still wanted to wait until after the baby was born so Angelo's child would have her maiden name instead of Steve's. She'd figure a way to handle it with Steve and the family later. But it was the one thing she could do to acknowledge, at least in her own mind, her love for her baby's father.

And she did love Angelo. Mafia or not. She had realized the fact of it much too late. She thought about him all the time. She missed him so much. She felt tears running down her face. "Where are you, my love?" she whispered.

*   *   *

Michael ate his Popeyes fried chicken automatically. It was Christmas and only one of his guards was here today. He heard the other say he would be in later after he played Santa Claus for his children. Michael couldn't imagine the quiet giant as the benevolent gift giver and he felt sorry for the poor children this man had spawned.

Not that "Brutus," the name Michael had given the guard, was unkind to him. Both of his jailers just treated him as if he didn't exist. He'd been in this hellhole for a month and a half, and Michael still knew nothing about the two of them, not even their names. The other one, "Phantom," was huge and had earned his nickname because despite his size, he moved like a ballerina, quick and graceful.

Michael had made no progress in his quest to escape. He still didn't know where he was. He spent his days reading his People magazines, talking to Tom, exercising off the couple of Popeyes' pounds he knew he'd gained, and staring out the tiny barred window in his small cell. In fact, he was looking out of it now, wondering for the hundredth time if an old unpainted building had been a grocery store at one time. The rotting structure was so close he felt he could reach out and touch it.

As he glanced out his window, he thought he saw smoke drifting from one of the holes in the side of the old building. In fact, he smelled smoke. Or, maybe it was just his imagination.

"Hey, fellow," he shouted to Phantom, "You smell smoke?"

Phantom left the jail in a hurried dance without responding. A few moments later, Michael could hear the scream of sirens in the distance. Before he could think about what was happening, yellow-clad firefighters with New Iberia Volunteer Fire Department printed on their bright red truck were chopping at his barred window with axes. "We're gonna save you. Don't worry," one shouted. "We're coming," his partner chimed in."

Before long, Michael was being pulled through the hole where the window once was.

"What were you doing in that old deserted jailhouse?" the young firefighter who looked about thirteen years old asked him.

"Deserted? Uh, it's a long story." Michael couldn't believe he was free. He glanced quickly around, but Phantom was nowhere in sight.

"Look, could you fellows give me a ride back to New Iberia?"

"Sure," the youngster said. "We're almost finished here. Damm kids. They come out here to smoke," he said lighting an unfiltered Camel. No parental supervision, that's the problem."

The four firefighters delegated Michael to the back of the truck because he smelled so bad. Besides, he looked deranged with his unshaven face and puffy, dark angry eyes. He kept glancing at his wrist to check the time, except he wasn't wearing a watch.

     *   *   *

A few hours after leisurely consuming a marvelous Christmas buffet luncheon, T.J. and Steve drove to the other side of town. Steve stopped at a beautifully restored raised cottage on the River.

"Wow, this place is great," T.J. said, looking appreciatively at the old Bergeron house that had become really run-down for a while after the aged sisters died when T.J. and Steve were kids. Who lives here now?"

"We do. I mean we could. If you like it, we could make an offer on it."

"But, what about your place. You love your house."

"My house is too small for the three of us. And, our other children."

"What other children?"

"Well, you always said you didn't like being an only child and you wanted lots of kids."

"Yeah, well right now, I feel like one is more than enough."

"Come on, I have a key," Steve said, pulling T.J. toward her future home. If she so chose. The two of them spent an hour exploring the house and grounds. There were five bedrooms, two down and three up. Plenty enough room for a growing family. The kitchen had been totally redone and even had a stainless built in sub-zero refrigerator. The landscaper had restored the Bergeron sisters' rose garden and T.J. could imagine the profusion of color when the flowers started blooming in the summer.

It was a little chilly to remain outside too long, so they walked back inside. Steve turned to T.J. and before he could ask, she replied. "OK. April 15."

"But, that's after the baby's…" Steve started to protest, then changed his mind. "All right. April 15, it is."

He took T.J. in his arms. "I love you."

"I love you, too," T.J. said and meant it.

*　　　　　　*　　　　　　*

T.J. was so big she was having trouble getting around. She had declined several invitations to New Year's Eve parties. She and Lawanna usually ushered in the new year by attending two or three private parties in New Orleans with or without dates. Tonight she had opted to stay in and prepare a romantic dinner for Steve and herself.

Lawanna was working the graveyard shift in the emergency room at Charity, since New Year's Eve was the busiest night of the year-the chalkboard showing numerous car accidents, shootings, stabbings. You name it. "Sadly, alcohol and people really don't mix well," Lawanna often lamented.

T.J. was making real Italian pasta. The kind with fresh tomatoes that you cooked all day. With big fat meatballs loaded with garlic. She was washing the lettuce for salad when the doorbell rang.

"Just in time," she called out, moving clumsily to the door. T.J. couldn't believe her eyes. Instead of her fiancée, Angelo stood there, his mouth agape as he took in his enormously pregnant love.

"T.J.?" It was almost a question.

"Angelo? Where have you been?"

"You're pregnant. Is it…?" he started to ask, but was interrupted by a voice behind him.

"Is it what?" Steve asked, staring at Angelo, trying not to show surprise at seeing him here.

"Steve, honey, do you remember Angelo?"

"Sure, I haven't seen you around lately," Steve said, recovering from the surprise and extending his hand.

"I've been out of town."

"On vacation?"

"Working."

Actually, when Michael had shared his crazy jail experience in Cajun Country with Mark O'Keefe, his supervisor had not seemed that surprised. "You did say the Marino girl told you that Colarossi knew you were one of us, didn't you?" he'd commented.

"Yes."

"This smells Mob. You should have been more careful," he had admonished before filling Michael in on some progress that had been made in his absence.

Now all Michael wanted to do was hug T.J. Take her in his arms and hold her gently. To pretend she was not obviously committed to this man who stood possessively with his arm around her. She was still wearing the engagement ring only. No wedding band.

"Have you set the date?" Michael asked inanely.

"April 15," Steve answered, squeezing T.J.'s shoulder.

"Tax day," Michael muttered.

T.J. was shocked into silence at seeing Angelo after all this time. She realized they were still standing in the doorway of her apartment. "Will you come in?" she asked.

"No, I really need to go," Michael said, realizing the futility of it all. He had lost the love of his life. The child she was carrying had to be Rose's. She would never marry another man if she was pregnant with his child. Never.

Chapter 17

Gatherings

The KC Hall in Tallula was packed for the town meeting. Everyone was always optimistic during the first official meeting of the new year, and Tony had his usual problems getting the crowd's attention so he could open the session.

Father Hebert was smoking full-time again. He started when his sister was in the hospital, and just a couple of months later was chain-smoking. To the disgust of Lou Ella Turner, he was actually smoking two cigarettes at the same time. The other members of the Council were fanning the smoke out of their eyes with their agenda sheets.

After the reading of the minutes by Miss Emmie and unanimous approval, Millie Washington gave the treasurer's report. The only remaining old business needing to be dealt with was the tax revolt issue. Usually after so many months, the people in Tallula were more forgiving of the government for taking such a big portion of their earnings.

Thoughts on the matter expressed tonight were no exception. A few IRS changes had been enacted during the year. No major reform or breaks, just enough hype about a gentler and kinder IRS so the citizens of the country might think the president and members of Congress had their best interest in mind.

Despite knowing that the folks would never stage a tax revolt, Tony felt obligated to take a vote on the matter.

"Hold on, before we vote, there's something I want to say." Doc Romero stood up. "I think we need to put an end to this tax revolt business. Year after year, we say we're gonna do something, but we get all riled up for nothing."

"Amen," Cora led half the group in approval of Doc Romero's wisdom.

"Wait a minute, Doc," Tom Walters said rising, "How about if we do something that's not drastic or illegal. Just make our unhappiness with the system known."

"Like what?" Viola Perkins asked, trying to boost her lover.

"I was thinking we could draw up a letter of protest."

Frankie Colarossi snickered, "You mean we write a note to Uncle Sam saying we think your tax system stinks?"

Everyone laughed politely out of respect for the old Don who they knew had cheated the system forever.

Tom was not intimidated. "Sure, except we say it nicer."

Sheriff Washington chipped in, "We say, 'Dear Sir, I'm gonna pay these darn taxes, but I don't like it one bit'."

"Or even better, 'Dear Sir, I'm gonna pay these fucking taxes, but I don't like it one fucking bit'," someone in the back of the hall muttered loud enough to be heard by Annie who didn't turn to see who'd uttered the filth, but crossed herself instead.

Tom, still pleased with his idea stood again to add, "We file our returns as usual. Except no one files early. We all wait 'til about two weeks before the April 15 deadline, attach the letter to the form and send it in."

"Are you crazy? I file early every year. I don't want those crooks keeping my refund one minute longer than they have to." This from the usually mild banker, L.J. La Deaux. Words of agreement could be heard throughout the room.

"Come on, for this to be effective, we need to do this as a group. You can wait a little longer for your money, can't you? "Tony chimed in, warming to Tom's idea.

"And suppose we say no," Cora asked.

"Come on Cora," Tony teased, "you haven't filed in years."

"But suppose I want to send the letter," Cora persisted.

"We just put your letter in with ours," Tony laughed, looking at Diana to make sure she thought this was OK, but Cora had already changed her mind.

"I don't really want to send no letter to the govement, I just want to be sure, if I did want to send one, I could, you see."

Everyone ignored Cora's ornery banter and discussion on the final form of the letter ensued. There seemed to be feeling that the although the letter would probably get lost in the bureaucracy, it didn't matter, because what was important was everyone in town who participated would finally be doing what they'd talked about doing for years, staging a tax protest. With little or no risk at all.

After everyone in attendance approved the motion to attach the letters to their returns, Tom volunteered to draft a rough version to be presented at next month's Council meeting. The new business on the agenda was dispensed with quickly.

The annual Clean the River Campaign planned and implemented by The Sisters was under way. Frances, clad in her black leather motorbike gear and with her young Boudreaux boyfriend hanging on, reported on its progress.

Emelda Walters announced she heard Walmart was coming to town. Emelda always shopped at the Dillards in the mall in Houma, and had said repeatedly she wouldn't dare set foot in a discount store. Everyone could tell, she could hardly wait for the new store to be built.

Most everybody stayed to socialize and nibble on homemade chocolate chip cookies and soft drinks.

*   *   *

The driveway in front of Fair Oaks was bursting with activity. Women carrying brightly covered packages were arriving every few minutes.

T.J.'s baby shower was being held in the large, informal Florida room near the back of the house with a view of the River. The room was big enough to accommodate T.J.'s friends from high school and college, as well as a couple of women from the law firm and numerous relatives, The Sisters and their friends.

Lawanna sat next to T.J. on a small striped loveseat. She had made plans a month ago so she could be here for the occasion. In fact, she and T.J. had driven down together and Lawanna planned to spend the night in Tallula. T.J. looked around the room. There must have been 100 women in attendance.

The hosts for the affair, Diana's sisters, sat in a stiff line-up on a large floral sofa that matched the loveseat across the room where T.J. visited with a crowd of women.

"She looks good, don't you think?" Lucie asked, waiting for the absent James to echo "good." She repeated the word herself.

"She looks like hell." Frances said in her usual forthright manner.

"You don't have to curse," Annie chided and crossed herself.

Cora set a large milk-glass bowl of green fruit punch down on the long table borrowed from the KC Hall and camouflaged with a white lace cloth, then went back to get a tray of finger-sandwiches.

"What do you mean about T.J.?" Lucie asked. "T.J."

"She looks swollen, puffy and not very happy."

"Well, you'd look a little miserable yourself if you were eight months pregnant and big as a house." Diana, who had entered the room with a plate of petit fours and overheard the conversation, was irritated by Frances' observations. Especially since she'd been thinking the same thing.

"Oh, Di. I don't mean to be critical. I'm just worried about T.J., that's all."

"Why? She may be doing all this a little backwards, but she is going to marry the town's most eligible bachelor."

"That's just it. If she loves him so much, how come she's waiting 'til after the baby comes to marry him? That doesn't sound like love to me.

Besides, I thought she was in love with John Conti. Are you sure the baby's not his? I mean, they were on a romantic cruise together."

"How could you think such evil thoughts?" Annie pulled out her rosary. She still prayed with it, despite her new, unorthodox religion.

"Look, Fran, T.J.'s a big girl."

"Very very big," Lucie said seriously. "Big."

They all laughed despite the seriousness of the conversation.

"Shit, I mean she's a grown woman."

"The language in this family's going to send everyone straight to hell." Annie made the sign of the cross with the crucifix of her rosary.

Cora who was bustling about trying to finish setting everything up, hovered close to The Sisters so she wouldn't miss a word of the little chat they were having.

"When's T.J. going to open the presents?" Lucie asked. "Presents." Lucie had begun having panic attacks when she was away from James and was trying to focus on something else besides the fact that her heart was starting to race to beat the band.

"After we play all those wonderful little shower games," Emelda Walters, approaching the clique, chimed in sweetly.

"Emelda, we're so glad you could make it. New dress?" Diana tried not to laugh seeing Tom's wife so overdressed as usual. This afternoon the obese woman wore an extremely short evening dress with sequins. Her white legs looked a lot like the two large pillars that graced the front of Fair Oaks.

Diana looked across the room at T.J. and her friends. Her sisters followed her glance. Each took out her Brookstone fan and despite the fact that it was the middle of January and comfortable in the mansion, they fanned themselves in unison.

Meanwhile on the other side of the room, T.J. tried to focus on the festivities being held in her honor. She was tired of being pregnant.

"I want my body back," she told Lawanna and anyone who would listen repeatedly. "I want my boobs to stop hurting. I want to touch my toes. Hell, I want to see my toes. Most of all I want to see my child. I want to hold my baby."

"Will you be living in your little apartment in New Orleans?" Millie Washington, ever practical, asked.

"No, I'm gonna stay with Mama and Daddy until the wedding."

"What about your job?"

"I'm going to work 'til the baby's born, then take leave for a few months after. I guess I'll need to start looking for something around here."

"What about going in with Tom Walters and John Conti?" Miss Emmie who had never married and adored wedding showers and baby showers made the suggestion.

"Is John back?" T.J. asked, curious about what had happened to him. The question was overheard by Frances and the other sisters who had moved toward T.J.'s side of the room in anticipation of the party games. Frances nodded knowingly and whispered to the others, "I told you."

"Not yet, but I heard from Lou Anne, you know Tom's secretary that he's coming back next week."

"Oh."

Frances read a lot in T.J.'s simple response.

After the games, T.J. opened gifts. She would not have to buy one thing for the baby. Her mama and aunts had been giving her gifts since the beginning. And now she was going to have the best dressed child in Louisiana with all these Baby Gaps and Ralph Laurens and Baby Diors. T.J. was tired. Happy, but tired.

She caught Lawanna's attention and smiled her contentment. Lawanna came over bringing her friend a glass of punch and a party plate filled with goodies.

"You doing OK?"

"I'm fine. Thanks for asking. For being here."

    *   *   *

Michael couldn't get T.J. out of his mind. He was crazy with jealousy, and he used the time he should have spent investigating his incarceration in Iberia Parish following Steve Rose instead. He was desperate to find out something about the doctor he could use to dissuade T.J. from marrying him. Instead, the man was near perfect. A model citizen, a good physician, totally devoted to T.J. despite his reputation as a womanizer prior to becoming engaged to his long-time friend.

"How in the hell can I compete with a damn saint," Michael said to himself as he pulled his truck full of chickens behind Rose's Jag. He was dressed like a chicken farmer with a large straw hat more appropriate to Northwest Arkansas than Southern Louisiana nearing the end of its sugar-making season. He could just see himself trying to keep up with the sleek Jaguar driving one of those huge, cumbersome cane trucks loaded to overflowing with the purple stalks headed for the sugar mills in the area. Better to be using his souped-up chicken truck even if he did have to ruffle a few feathers. Michael chuckled out loud at his own corny play on words.

Steve Rose seemed to be headed for New Orleans, which was a little unusual being it was the middle of the week and still fairly early in the afternoon. He was in no hurry though. Probably just going to check on T.J. who must be getting close to delivery. He really hadn't asked when the baby was due.

He didn't even want to think about it. Michael spent the hour and a half trip listening to the radio and thinking. He stayed at a comfortable distance behind Rose. Elvis was singing Jailhouse Rock and Michael's thoughts immediately moved from T.J. to his jail escapade. He was pretty sure the Mafia had been behind his imprisonment, but he had no proof.

He had gone to the State Troopers headquarters, but no one there knew anyone who met the description of the so-called arresting officer. Nor were there any arrest orders for him. The troopers usually gave out tickets anyway for traffic violations or so he was told. This, despite a lot of bad press in the past about Louisiana law enforcement officers illegally stopping and arresting travelers on bogus charges, then confiscating their property.

Michael followed Rose across the narrow Huey P. Long Bridge. The lanes hardly seemed large enough to accommodate the wide truck with feathers flying everywhere. Instead of exiting Claiborne Ave. when he reached the French Quarter, Steve continue on the interstate toward Slidell. Michael was surprised to find himself on Rigolets Road not far from where he and Mark O'Keefe and other members of the FBI task force were scheduled to meet this evening.

He watched as Steve turned into the small parking lot of a deserted restaurant and drove around the back. Michael continued a short distance on Rigolets before stopping. He parked the truck on the narrow shoulder, told the squawking chickens to be quiet, pulled his straw hat down over his eyes and approached the restaurant.

*   *   *

Steve was angrier than he had ever been. No one seated around the table could look him in the eyes.

"What happened?"

"Boss, I heard there was a fire and he was rescued by the New Iberia fire department," Frankie Modella volunteered bravely.

"I know that. But why?"

"Cause that's their job, to save burning buildings and people in them?" Frankie was amused by the whole thing and his flippant answer just popped out. Luckily, Steve chose to ignore Frankie's suicidal retort.

"Did they find out who he was and what he was doing there?"

"Nah. One of the **guardie** was watching from behind the bushes and he said Deluca didn't say a word. The guard said he saw Deluca hitch a ride with them and watched as he called somebody from the New Orleans bureau to pick him up. So we lucked out."

"Maybe. Why didn't those two jackals get him out of there before the firemen arrived?"

"It was Christmas," John Sabatori, the brains of the small group of elderly hoodlums, offered.

"I see. What in the hell does Christmas have to do with anything?"

"One of the guards had to play Santa to his bambinos."

"I want them punished."

"You want I should off the jokers? I'd be glad to take them out and I don't mean to dinner if you git my drift." Joey Romano spoke for the first time. He'd done his job and was in no trouble with the young Don.

"Thanks Joey. But I need you to take care of Deluca. Frankie, why don't you take a little trip to Cajun Country and have a conversation with the two idiots. Bring some muscle, but don't hurt them too much. Especially Santa."

"Anything you say, Boss, but word is those two fellows have relocated to Houston which is the same as disappearing from the face of the earth."

"Try."

"Sure, Boss."

"Joey, I'll get back to you later."

*   *   *

Michael could barely make out the faces sitting around the table in the deserted restaurant, despite the fact that it was still daylight. The window hadn't been cleaned in years. What were they doing? Playing poker? Rose was involved with illegal gambling? There were lots of little poker parties in Tallula. He didn't need to come all the way here in the middle of the afternoon in the middle of the week to play. A busy doctor. Of course, maybe he played poker instead of golf on his Thursday afternoons off.

Michael moved to another window that appeared a little bit cleaner. He could see much better. Well enough, in fact, to realize that Steve

Rose was with several old men and there were no cards on the table before them. And that one of Rose's companions was the old man who had shadowed him prior to his so-called arrest. As he watched the group rise and head for the door, Michael moved quickly from the window and back to the truck, more puzzled than ever.

*   *   *

"You say you saw the same old man you accosted on Canal Street with Dr. Rose and three other unsavory-looking guys. All over seventy? In an abandoned restaurant? Down the road?"

"Look, Mark." Michael faced O'Keefe and five other **suits** who were helping out with the Naughty Games task force. Michael had not bothered to change and the others were trying not to laugh as the young chicken farmer described the puzzling scene he had witnessed earlier.

"Something fishy was going on, I tell you."

"Well, Mike," O'Keefe said, suddenly dead serious, "let me tell you about what Mr. Joseph Romano's been up to lately."

"Who?"

"The old fellow with the bullshit story about his relative being done in by the Mob. You know, the one you had the little heart to heart with in front of Maison Blanche."

O'Keefe pulled out a blown-up photo of Michael and Joey as well as a couple of Times-Picayune articles describing Romano's arrest and the untimely death of one of New Orleans' finest.

"Well, I'll be dammed. This is wonderful."

"You get set up by the Mob and all you have to say is 'this is wonderful'?"

"I mean. Steve Rose is the one. I can't believe it."

"Believe it. Now, let's get something on him more convincing than an afternoon tea with some old ladies on Rigolets."

"I won't leave his side 'til we can put him away. You can count on it."

Chapter 18

Mama Mia

T.J. was gambling again. She was so big she could hardly fit on the stool in front of the slot machine. She put three quarters in and watched as the three sevens lined up. She wasn't sure how much she won until that yellow light on the top of her machine started flashing and screaming. Quarters were pouring out of the machine, faster than she could scoop them up with her cup. They were spilling all over the floor and down the aisle where jubilant gamblers were scrambling after them, slipping and sliding.

"No", T.J. shouted, "this isn't supposed to be happening. They're supposed to give me a check." The baby she was carrying wasn't happy with all the smoke and the noise and started kicking T.J. Really hard.

T.J. woke holding her stomach. She was really hurting, but the baby wasn't due for two more weeks. Probably the false labor pains she was always hearing about. T.J. looked at the clock. It was after 6 a.m.

She thought about the dream. She obviously hadn't gotten over her gambling addiction. Of course, lots of members in Gamblers Anonymous dreamed of gambling. Even though it felt like she'd slipped, she hadn't really. Still, she had had so much fun winning the jackpot. Which she'd never done in real life. Maybe it was just a dream, but she felt guilty anyway.

It was too late to go back to sleep and her stomach was still hurting a little bit, so T.J. decided to get up and get in to the office early for a change. She showered and had a light breakfast of Cheerios and milk with a banana. She dressed in a maternity business suit with a short skirt to show off her shapely legs. She was so big and her feet so swollen, she couldn't find a pair of shoes to wear. So, she slipped on the moose slippers Lawanna had given her for Christmas, grabbed her attaché case and headed for the office.

*   *   *

About 10 a.m., T.J. sat at her desk waiting for her next client, Jenny Chauvin, who was running a few minutes late as usual. T.J. was still cramping every once in a while. Like every hour or so, but she kept telling herself it wasn't time yet. Not like Jenny who was already two weeks late and was so uncomfortable she could barely move around.

Her secretary, a temp who couldn't figure out the phone system, stuck her head in the doorway to notify T.J. that her appointment was here. A few minutes later the two pregnant women faced each other.

Jenny had come to T.J. at the beginning of her pregnancy because she was being terminated from her social worker job at one of the local hospitals and they refused to give her severance pay. The case had dragged on forever and now it looked like they were finally willing to settle. For a year's severance pay. Which was pretty stupid and costly for the hospital when all Jenny wanted was a few months compensation.

But the hospital administrator was angry with Jenny for hinting there might be a few things that corporate compliance would be interested in knowing. Particularly the pats on the butt that he insisted were friendly. At the time Jenny had just found out she was pregnant and didn't want to get entangled in a long, sexual harassment suit, so instead decided to resign with severance.

The administrator convinced the VP of the company Jenny didn't deserve severance even though she had been there for five years. Instead, he wanted to fire her for cause, pointing out that she was not doing her social assessments in a timely manner and that "being pregnant was really going to put a damper on her already poor performance."

"Sit down, Jenny. I have good news," T.J. said.

Jenny tried to sit in one of the leather chairs facing T.J.'s desk but it was low and she couldn't manage the maneuver.

"I'd better stand."

"Me too."

The two women stood facing each other, bellies almost touching, until T.J. moved behind her desk.

"Jenny, they want to settle for a bundle. Ouch!"

"How big a bundle? Wow!"

"Wow? I have not even told you how much yet."

"I just had a pain. You said 'ouch.' You too?"

"It's nothing," T.J. said. "Just a little cramping now and then. You need to call your doctor?"

"I have been to the hospital five times already with false labor. I am not going back 'til I can see the color of my son's hair."

T.J. laughed. "You know it's going to be a boy?"

"Yeah, I was so curious there was no way I could wait nine months to find out. You still don't know?"

T.J. shook her head.

"No, but I'm just about ready to find out." "Wow," she added clutching her stomach as a stronger pain took her breath away. "You think I'd better call my doctor?"

"No. I tell you. This is your first child. Even if you are in labor, it should take at least twelve hours before the baby comes."

"Sure," T.J. said. "So, what are you going to do with a year's worth of salary in one lump sum?"

"How much?" Jenny screamed. "I've got to be in labor."

"Hold on, let me get some help." T.J. buzzed her secretary.

The young woman whose name she'd forgotten was away from the desk, so T.J. ran out and shouted for help.

Several attorneys and their clients rushed out of offices to find out what was happening. One attorney volunteered to get Jenny to the hospital, another to call her husband and one to notify her physician that she was on her way.

By this time, T.J. was in constant pain herself. She called her obstetrician who was on vacation and was told his on-call replacement would get back to her as soon as possible.

T.J. could feel wetness running down her legs. "Oh, I've peed in my pants," she said out loud. Her secretary who had returned from a thirty-minute break stuck her head in the door to see if T.J. was talking to her.

"Uh, what's your name again?"

"Eloise."

"OK, Eloise, here's the thing. I'm having a baby."

"Yes, Madam, I could tell."

"Eloise. I'm having this baby now. So, what should I do?"

Eloise took one look at T.J., then ran out of the room yelling, "help." The same attorneys, minus the one who had taken Jenny to the hospital came running again.

One of T.J.'s co-workers, a mother of two and recent grandmother for the first time, got T.J. to lie down on the sofa. She covered her with one of Grandma Connie's polyester afghans and had her raise her skirt. She thought she might be seeing the baby's head, but couldn't be sure.

Meanwhile, the obstetrician called back. He didn't think T.J. had time to get uptown to Baptist Hospital, so asked that T.J meet him at Charity instead. The hospital where Lawanna worked was only a few blocks away from the renovated law office on Chartes near Canal.

T.J. was shrieking now. "Call Dr. Lewis and tell her I'm coming. Her number's in my cardex. Hurry, Eloise. Hurrrie!"

*   *   *

Lawanna waited anxiously near the emergency room entrance. She watched as a Checker Cab pull up and a young woman obviously in the process of delivering her baby emerged. As if sensing her presence, an ER team immediately appeared and placed her on a Gurney, then whisked her away to delivery if she had time.

Lawanna had heard stories about how in the old days, women never feared being turned away from Charity if they didn't have physicians or pre-natal care as long as they arrived in the last stages of labor. Lots of babies were delivered by cab drivers, or if they were lucky, by emergency room student nurses.

But why in the world was her friend coming to Charity? The young woman who'd called Lawanna was hysterical. She kept yelling something about it being her first day on the job and no one told her she was going to be dealing with all these pregnant women.

Surely the caller wasn't T.J.'s obstetrician's nurse, Lawanna thought. All the young doctor understood from the woman who phoned her, was something about "Mrs. Marino's baby coming out" so she was supposed to "call this number and tell Dr. Lewis that Mrs. Marino was on her way to Charity" and that's all she knew.

A few minutes later, a big black Mercedes drove up. T.J. was helped out by a gray haired youthful looking woman. Lawanna took one look at her friend and knew why she was at Charity. She confiscated a Gurney from a surprised orderly who was waiting for an approaching ambulance.

"Help me get her up here, Joe," Lawanna shouted over the sound of the ambulance's siren.

"It's gonna be OK, Tee," Lawanna soothed. "My Godchild is almost here, and I'm going to help bring her into the world."

T.J. let out a scream and Lawanna laughed. "Hey, I've done this before, trust me." T.J. screamed again.

T.J. had been transferred to a hospital bed in a small cubicle in the emergency room. Lawanna barely had time to issue instructions to the nurses to notify Steve Rose and T.J.'s parents who had planned to be with her during the delivery. The baby's head was beginning to emerge and Lawanna grabbed a pair of gloves and told T.J. what was happening.

"You want me to push?"

"Push? Why? The kid's here."

Just about that time, T.J. heard a lusty cry and said excitedly, "I had a boy, didn't I? Let me see him."

"One moment," Lawanna said as she cut the cord, "and you'll get to hold your daughter."

T.J. had been moved to a ward. The on-call physician had arrived after the birth and wanted to transfer her to Baptist, but T.J. was doing fine and asked if she could stay overnight. Lawanna made the arrangements and here she was with a slew of new mothers holding her precious Angel. Angeline. The perfect name for the perfect baby.

She and Steve had tentatively decided to name the child Josie after his grandmother and call her Jo if it was a girl. Maybe they could call her Angeline Josie Rose. Didn't sound that great. Not nearly as nice as Angeline Deluca.

"Stop thinking like that," T.J. told herself as her parents entered the ward.

A couple of hours later, Diana took in the crowded, dingy ward and started to frown. Then she saw the baby in T.J.'s arms and melted. There were congratulations and tears of joy. Tony was so happy. T.J. had been in labor for only six hours and apologized to her parents for not giving them more notice.

Steve, who had been performing a tonsillectomy in Morgan City when the call came, rushed in. T.J. put the baby in his arms. She wiped away tears of happiness and regret as Steve held the baby. T.J. wanted to tell him that the baby was not his. She had started to tell him several times before, but she couldn't hurt him. She just couldn't. She loved him too much.

Lawanna stopped in before going off duty to check on T.J. and her Godchild. She held the child she had delivered a few hours before. The baby had dark hair and the dark blue eyes of a lot of newborns. She looked just like T.J. and as Lawanna held her best friend's baby to her heart, mother and friend gave each other congratulatory smiles.

"You did good, Tee," Lawanna said.

"You did good, too. Thanks," T.J. answered.

       *   *   *

Around the time Diana and Tony Marino were oohing and aahing over their first grandchild, Michael Zello adjusted the James Decon, MD nametag on his white lab coat and followed Steve Rose to the elevators in the lobby of the massive hospital. He had been tailing the young doctor almost constantly now and couldn't imagine that Rose treated patients at this hospital. Michael figured he must be visiting someone, probably an old classmate of his.

He watched as Rose greeted a young black woman also dressed in a white lab coat in front of the elevator. He could not make out the name on her badge, but she looked familiar. He was standing behind a group of student nurses, trying not to look too conspicuous when he heard the young woman say, "Tell T.J. I'll be up in a little bit."

T.J.? What was T.J. doing here? Was she having the baby? Surely she could afford to deliver her baby at any of the fine private hospitals in New Orleans. Michael didn't need to risk following Steve Rose as he entered the elevator. He headed for the information desk.

A short while later, Michael with his head averted, passed by the maternity ward where T.J. and her parents smiled proudly at the pink bundle being held gingerly in Steve Rose's arms. Michael felt sick so he headed for the doctor's lounge. He sat on a battered vinyl sofa for what seemed like ages. No one entered the drab room where even in the age of smokeless medical professionals, the large plastic ashtray overflowed with smelly cigarette butts.

Michael had been counting the weeks since he and T.J. made love. He figured if T.J. was a virgin, and the baby was a couple of weeks early, chances are it was his, not Steve Rose's. Suddenly, he had this mad desire to see the child.

Sometime later Michael Zello, alias Angelo Deluca, stood before the glass nursery window and gazed upon Baby Marino and knew the truth. Hadn't his Mom shown him enough of his own baby pictures to see the resemblance? It made no sense to Michael that T.J. would not marry him just because he worked for the FBI. She would marry a Mafiosa instead. Why? He knew T.J. loved him as much as he loved her. He looked at the baby. His baby. "I love you, kid," he whispered to the sleeping child. "I love you."

Chapter 19

Steve's Secret Life

"Dr. Rose, do you think I should take those new diet pills?" Emelda Walters asked. "I mean with all those people getting heart trouble from them. Maybe I could just go back to Weight Watchers?"

"Mrs. Walters." Steve always called her by her surname and she always called him Doctor, despite their having known each other forever. "No diet pills. Look, why don't you start exercising, like I've been telling you to do for years."

Steve didn't want to have to deal with Emelda's obesity today. He had other things on his mind. Like T.J. and the baby. Angie was almost a month old and the wedding was set for next month. On the surface, everything seemed to be going well.

Still Steve had the feeling, T.J. didn't really want to get married. That maybe she was just willing to make it legal because of their baby. She was staying at Fair Oaks with her parents instead of with him and had absolutely refused to have sex with him. When he pushed her, she pointed at little Angie as if to say, see what happens when you screw around.

T.J. wasn't the only thing that was bothering him these days. Ever since the Angelo Deluca thing had gone sour, he felt on edge. He was fairly sure Deluca and the Feds didn't have a clue as to his Mafia connections; still he was nervous that an angry Angelo might push a bit harder in getting something on the Louisiana Mob. Surely he knew by now that they had something to do with his incarceration during the holidays.

"Dr. Rose, are you all right?" Emelda tried to sound concerned, but she really didn't give a darn about the condition of the young physician. He was no help whatsoever. She ought to find a doctor in Houma like she'd been meaning to do for years.

"I'm fine, Mrs. Walters. Now your blood pressure's too high, so try hard to drop a few pounds," Steve said dismissing the ornery woman.

Emelda was the last patient of the day and he had to meet with the others tonight. He promised his Godfather that he would stop by before he left for Slidell. He hadn't visited the old Don in months making only necessary contact by phone. Pay phone using an alias. But he wanted to talk about T.J. He heard Johnnie was back in town. Maybe that had something to do with T.J.'s reluctance to march down the aisle. Frankie would tell him.

Frankie Colarossi. Steve Rose's Godfather. The murderer of Steve's own father. Or so he suspected. His mother never talked about it. But he didn't get to be head of the Louisiana Mafia by being stupid. Over the years, Steve put a scenario together that rivaled that of any of the popular Godfather movies.

Steve only suspected that his father, Luke Roselina, who died suspiciously in Chicago when Steve was still in diapers so to speak, had had a contract put out on him. A contract that originated in Louisiana by his own Godfather.

Why else would the old man have gone to the trouble to bring him and his Mama to South Louisiana and care for them so diligently? Granted the old Don was known to have a strong code of ethics when it came to family, especially to women and children. He probably felt it was his duty to take care of the kid he'd orphaned.

Steve never knew for sure and in a way he was glad. Because if he did find out that Frankie Colarossi was the one who ordered the early demise of his father, then he would have to avenge his father's death.

He would have to kill Frankie and he didn't want to do that. Partly because he had never killed anyone, but mostly because he had become fond of the old Mafiosa over the years.

On the day that Frankie told Steve he was to be his successor when he retired, Steve knew he would never try to find out what really happened to his father. Steve was just out of medical school. He'd always wanted to be a doctor and decided he could do both. Members of the Mob were lawyers, businessmen, even elected officials. But no doctors. He could do what he loved and still take care of "family" business. He never felt his two professions conflicted. Having to make your bones by offing someone like in the old days no longer was a factor.

Steve saved lives, he didn't take them. At least not on purpose. There were times when he lost patients. But only those who no one could have saved. He didn't kill them. Of course there were those like Emelda Walters who he always felt like killing.

Steve let himself into Frankie Colarossi's through his secret entrance and headed for the old man's study. It was so dark he couldn't find Frankie until he heard him clear his throat. He was seated behind his desk without his usual props and was almost completely hidden by the desk.

"Godfather?"

"Stephano, come closer so I can see you."

Steve greeted his mentor with a kiss on each cheek.

The two men spent some time talking about the state of things. The newest slot machine acquisitions and sales. The status of the FBI investigation, especially the Angelo Deluca threat. Finally Steve got down to the business most on his mind.

"I'm getting married on the 15th of April"

"Tax day."

"Yeah. T.J. said the whole thing started on April 15 last year and she has kind of a warped sense of humor."

"What'sa matter?"

"Something doesn't feel right. I heard Johnnie's back."

"So?"

"So you think she has a thing for him?"

"Nay. She told me early on she was gonna marry you."

"She told you? When?"

"A while back."

"She's been talking about going to work with Johnnie and Tom Walters after the baby's old enough, so I just thought maybe she...anyway, the wedding's soon."

"And the bambino?"

"Great."

"Good, I did'n know," Frankie shrugged.

*   *   *

It wasn't as cold as it had been and T.J. had the baby out on the patio for the first time. Of course Angie was bundled a bit more than necessary. First Mama had put a knit sweater and cap on top of the warm cotton outfit T.J. had dressed Angie in, then Cora had run upstairs and came back with a heavy wool blanket.

Angie was sitting in her stroller with the hood pulled down to protect her from the wind. It was almost seventy degrees and Angie was red as a beet, but T.J. figured Mama and Cora knew more than she did about taking care of a baby.

T.J. pulled the stroller over to the swing and put Angie on her lap.

"This is the swing that your daddy and I used to swing on. A long time ago. Well, not your real daddy, but the daddy who's gonna be your daddy."

Angie smiled at her Mama. T.J. smiled back.

"Can her real daddy hold her?"

"Angelo, you heard. This is Angie. Short for Angeline."

"Hi Angie," Michael said, taking the bundle in his arms and removing the blanket and outer clothing.

"She's beautiful. She looks like me," he said.

"Actually she's gorgeous. She looks more like me."

T.J. and Michael looked longingly at each other for a long time, then at their baby. Michael kissed Angie on her head and put her back in the stroller. He sat down next to T.J. on the swing, close, but not quite touching. Still T.J. could feel the heat from his body.

"Why did you come?" she asked. "Don't you realize how hard it is for me to want you so badly, knowing we can never be together?"

"But that's why I'm here. If it means you'll marry me, I'll give up my career."

"You'd do that? But how? You can't exactly go in and say, I quit." T.J. remembered how in **The Godfather**, Michael Corleone tried at first to disassociate himself from the Mafia, but his sense of family, of obligation to his father was too strong.

She knew Angelo was offering the ultimate sacrifice, perhaps even a dangerous one and she could not ask him to do that. "Angelo, I love you, but..."

Michael stopped her with a tender kiss. So tender it hurt.

"I love you, too" Suddenly they were kissing each other with desire that had grown greater than when they had conceived Angie.

"I need you so much," they said at the same time.

"I can't believe you're carrying on like this in front of your child." Cora appeared from nowhere and grabbed the baby's stroller pushing it haughtily away toward the house.

Your child? T.J. suspected all along that Cora knew and now she was sure. Cora wasn't stupid. She'd been there that first time. Never-the-less if Cora questioned why T.J. was practically making love to the strange fellow who rose out of the river that day almost a year ago, she didn't let on.

Michael laughed, but T.J. was mortified. "Angelo, listen. Steve and I are getting married on the 15th of next month."

"I know. But you don't love him. You love me. I'm willing to give up everything I love and have worked for since I was a kid for you." As soon as the words left his lips, Michael regretted them.

"That's what I thought," T.J. answered sadly. "I can't ask you to do that."

"But you're more important than anything," Michael argued. However, it was too late. The damage had been done.

"Will you at least think about it? Please."

"OK, I'll think about it." The two lovers looked at each other, each knowing the depths of hopelessness like they had never felt before. They gave each other a long, heartbreaking kiss, then Michael left. "Just think about it," he repeated softly.

Michael had been tempted to tell T.J. about Steve Rose, but professionally and ethically, he knew he could not. Not yet, but soon, it would all be out in the open. The wedding was only a month off, so he hoped it wouldn't be too late.

Chapter 20

The Letter

Dear Sir:

Please be advised that I believe the tax system in the Country stinks. The rates are much too high, the forms much too complicated and the collection system too much like the Gestapo. In other words, the entire IRS is in dire need of a complete overhaul.

Once again, I am filing my federal taxes under extreme duress. I hope this letter is brought to the attention of the proper authorities.

Sincerely and patriotically yours,

"Duress? What duress? We're getting a $4,000 refund this year."

"Shut up, Emelda," Tom hissed, and at the same time, smiled at Julius Green and Miss Emmie who were just arriving.

The letter was being passed around at an open house in a large viewing room of Breaux's Funeral Parlor. The KC Hall was being painted and this was the only private room large enough to handle the expected letter-signing crowd.

Besides, there hadn't been a funeral in ages and Gaston Long was getting a little antsy. He was only truly happy when he was consoling some poor souls with his pat, well-rehearsed words of condolence.

Gaston looked like a funeral director, so he tried extra hard not to. His ruddy complexion from too many visits to the tanning booth only called to everyone's attention that he was the exact caricature of one. Gaston was a tall, cadaverous, ashen fellow always dressed in a worn black suit. The only other strange thing about Gaston is he wore his fingernails long. So long, in fact, they were beginning to curl. So Gaston handed out the letters with a sad little practiced nod.

A caterer hired with funds accumulated by the Social Committee was passing out seafood canapés. The Mayor had donated beer and soft drinks hoping for a festive mood. Instead, everyone spoke in hushed tones, appropriate to the somber funeral parlor ambience.

The people were seated in folding chairs facing the coffin. Old Julius' masterpiece had been brought out two weeks early for the occasion and was on a platform in the front of the room.

"I feel like I need to go out and buy a black wreath to place in front of the coffin," Frances whispered to her sisters.

"Hush," Annie scolded.

"Why? You think there's a body up there?"

"I really am having second thoughts." Lucie said.

"Second thoughts." James echoed.

"For God's sake," Frances started to chastise Lucie for being so damn cautious, but changed her mind. Her phobic sister seldom attended public functions and Frances wanted to encourage each small step.

"Don't take the Good Lord's name in vain." Annie admonished Frances. Annie didn't quite know what to make of her younger sister. Since Johnny died, the woman had gone wild. Going straight to hell with all her gambling and carrying on with that Boudreaux fellow who was young enough to be her son. Riding that motorbike. Dressing like a street woman. And just last week, having her nose pierced like some rebellious teenager. Annie feared for Frances' mortal soul.

Frances looked at Annie. Heaven knows I love the woman, she thought, but what a kook she turned out to be. It was bad enough when she turned holy-roly. But this space ship cult is ridiculous.

Annie told everyone she had a little bag all packed to go when the "big ship" landed to pick up the good people to take them to Heaven, some distant, never heard of planet paradise that only true believers would ever see. According to Annie, everyone else was destined for Hell, another unknown, dark planet that was hot. Hotter, she was fond of telling Fran, than her worse hot flash. That was hard for Fran to imagine.

Fran touched the diamond stud in her nose. It's a good thing Annie didn't know about the other two piercings. She smiled to herself, thinking how horrified her sister would be if she said, "Let me show you something," and revealed the tiny rings she now wore in her navel and especially, her left nipple. Tim went crazy over that one.

"What are you grinning at?" Diana asked.

"Nothing in particular." Of course, she could have told Diana. Diana was the strong, stable one. At least she was until menopause struck a few years ago and ruined her idyllic life. Diana became neurotic as hell. Moody and mean one moment. Tearful and clinging the next. Now all that was changing. Either the estrogen patches were finally kicking in or that sweet little granddaughter was giving her a reason to forget her misery and to get up smiling in the morning.

"This letter is somewhat amateurish. Did we have to use the word stinks?" Viola Perkins didn't want to question her lover's work, but she also didn't want to sign anything that was less than professional. She was, after all, Tallula's only librarian and the people looked to her for intellectual correctness.

"We wanted to get their attention," Tom whined, hurt by her apparent desertion. He turned to a group that had approached to hear the lovers' spat. He thought they wanted to hear his defense of the letter, and so an hour later, he was still promoting his masterpiece to them and several others who had joined the group.

The letter-signing party had started at 5 p.m. and would run 'til midnight. T.J. and Steve arrived at about 10 p.m. T.J. had been reluctant to leave the baby with anyone but Diana. So, with much reservation, she had reluctantly left Angie in Cora's care.

Cora had decided the letter to the IRS was the work of the devil and didn't want to have anything to do with it. Besides, she didn't get a lot of chances to baby-sit because Miz Marino was always available. Cora was proud that T.J. trusted her enough to leave Angie with her while she and Dr. Rose attended the party.

"Let me tell you about the baby Jesus," Cora cooed to the happy infant as soon as T.J. and Dr. Rose walked out the door. "HE was born in a stable..."

There weren't too many people left by the time T.J. and Steve arrived at the Funeral Home. The coffin was almost full and was just being closed as the young couple entered the hall. T.J. spotted her parents talking with Tom Walters and Emelda Walters and guided Steve over toward them.

         *   *   *

Michael had followed T.J. and Steve Rose until they turned into the parking lot in front of Breaux's Funeral Parlor. "Who died?" he wondered aloud, planning his next move.

He decided to drive to Canata's supermarket in Morgan City. It was still open and although the florist was not on duty, he was able to purchase two large yellow mums. He bought a Saints baseball cap and turned it around. His leather jacket might be a little too expensive for a deliveryman, but it was an unusually chilly evening for April in South Louisiana and he would have to chance it.

He got back to Breaux's about 10:30 and entered a small vestibule. The heavy double doors leading to the viewing hall were suddenly opened by a large black man in a sheriff's uniform with a petite, pretty woman by his side. The woman smiled at Michael, but the man gave him a questioning look, started to say something, then thought about it and left without a word. When they were outside, Sheriff Washington asked Millie if she found it strange.

"What?"

"I haven't seen that guy around here before. Have you?"

"What guy?"

"That fellow in that expensive bomber jacket delivering flowers at this time of night."

"Maybe there's a funeral tomorrow."

"Who died?" the sheriff asked his wife.

"I don't know. I said 'maybe.' I suppose we'd have heard if someone died. No one ever dies around here. Not that I'm complaining."

"Humph. Something fishy is going on. I smell a rat."

"Right, and there's something rotten in Denmark."

"That, too," he added, then laughed along with Millie.

Not only did folks seldom die in Tallula, but nothing exciting ever happened. So the deliveryman was probably supposed to be at one of the other funeral homes in the area. And that jacket? Maybe the man owned the florist shop, the sheriff thought. Hell, maybe he owned a whole bunch of florist shops in another parish.

*   *   *

Michael had pulled the mums up to hide his face and he breathed a sigh of relief as he peeked through the doors that now stood ajar. There were about twenty or so people in the room in several small groups. They obviously didn't care about the poor dead person because no one was paying the slightest bit of attention to whoever was closed up in that gaudy pine box.

What was that carved in the coffin? Cows with horns? Bulls? As he edged closer, he realized it was deer with huge antlers. He had planned to carry the flowers to the platform and hide behind the numerous other funeral wreaths that usually stood before the coffin. But this poor soul obviously didn't have any friends.

There wasn't even one single flower adorning the coffin. Michael took a deep breath and moved to the front of the room. He placed the two potted plants down in front of the coffin. He realized that someone was laughing. He glanced down from the platform to the first row. An old man dressed all in black was seated there flanked by several younger men also dressed in black. Must be the family of the deceased, Michael thought, then wondered if he should go offer his condolences.

The small group seemed to think he was funny. **Stupida**. Michael heard the old man wheeze the word to even louder laughter that seemed to be attracting the attention of others in the room.

Michael saw in a flash that Steve Rose had turned to see what was happening. T.J. had her back to him, and before she could turn around he stepped down and headed for the door. He glanced back and saw Rose move toward the group in the front row. When he thought no one was watching, Rose quickly whispered something to the older fellow who turned to look in his direction. It dawned on Michael that the old guy must be Frankie Colarossi, the elusive and reclusive South Louisiana Mafiosa boss who didn't look anything like his pictures.

No wonder there weren't any flowers up there. Probably some small time hood wiped out by one of his own kind. Well, important enough to have his wake attended by Colarossi and Rose. Yeah, important, but definitely not too well-liked.

Although no one seemed to be following him, Michael moved quickly toward the exit, glancing back over his shoulder to make sure.

He nearly knocked over a strange looking fellow with a sunburn, said "excuse me" and hurried out the door.

Gaston righted himself indignantly and entered the viewing hall. He noticed the flowers and hurried to the front of the room. "Oh, aren't they lovely. Is there a card?" he asked, getting into his funeral director role, forgetting for the moment this wasn't really a funeral. The small group left was laughing hysterically by this time. All except Steve Rose.

He needed to act quickly to get rid of Deluca. No more messing with the small-time idiots. The man was becoming too brazen. Too much of a threat to the business. And definitely too much of a threat to him.

Chapter 21

Gatherings: Part 11

T.J. looked around the room, tears streaming down her face. Surrounded by family and friends, and yet not one person tried to console her. T.J. knew they didn't even know why she was crying. Could be tears of joy as far as they were concerned.

Most of the same people who attended the baby shower were here for the bridal shower, the third in two weeks. Except for Lawanna. She couldn't make it. She had been in Tallula last week for the housewares shower. T.J. wished her friend were here. She would know how to make her laugh at her predicament. If you could call marrying her best friend whom she loved dearly a predicament.

Victoria's Secret had made a killing. T.J. looked at the pile of sexy black, purple and Redlight-District-scarlet lingerie and wondered what it would be like to be as hooker.

More tears fell.

Cora brought her a crystal cup filled to the brim with a fruit punch of some sort. Cora looked disdainfully at the sinful-looking pieces of clothing, picked up the only Granny gown, a gift from Annie and covered the pile with it. She walked on without a word.

Diana came over and chatted with T.J. about the turnout and all the fun gifts, totally ignoring her daughter's tears. So did several of her friends. No one bothered to ask why she was crying. Everyone figured T.J.'s hormones were raging.

Angie was asleep in the library. It was the baby's favorite room in the whole mansion. Something about the musty, old books lulled her to sleep even when she was cranky. Every once in a while, T.J. would get up and peek in on her to make sure she was OK.

The wedding was just a week away and everything was ready. She would wear a simple ivory dress with a beautiful train made by Miss Crawford, a local woman in her seventies who made Mardi Gras ball gowns for the socialites in New Orleans. It had taken hours for the old seamstress to hand-sew hundreds of faux pearls onto the bodice of the silk gown.

Frances' favorite caterer from Franklin had been hired. And a small unknown group of musicians from Morgan City, the Seawall Slickers, would play at the reception that was going to be held on the lawn at Fair Oaks. Unless it rained.

Father Hebert would perform the ceremony at the tiny church where T.J.'s parents had married over thirty years ago. Her Uncle Robert, who had sung at her parent's wedding so many years ago still had a beautiful voice and would sing at hers. Her favorite, "Ave Maria." In Italian, no less.

Just thinking about marching down the aisle with her beaming daddy brought new tears to her eyes. What am I going to do? T.J. wondered.

The Sisters walked up and each gave her a little peck on the cheek. Lucie and Annie ignored the tears, but Frances who all along felt something wasn't right about this marriage, decided to confront her niece.

"You love the other fellow, don't you, honey?" she whispered, adjusting her tight lime mini skirt.

"Oh, Aunt Fran, I wish I didn't."

"Why aren't you...come with me." Frances brought T.J. to the library where the baby was still asleep.

"Why aren't you marrying him then?"

"I can't. He's in the Mob."

"Look, just because he's Frankie Colarossi's grandson doesn't nec-essarily mean he's in the Mafia."

"Grandson? Angelo's Frankie Colarossi's grandson, too? I thought he was his Godson."

"Angelo? Who's Angelo?"

"The man I love. Who are you talking about?"

"John Conti."

"Oh, no. John's...Johnnie's just a friend."

"Well, who's this Angelo?"

T.J. hadn't told anyone in the family about Angelo. That he was Angie's father, that he was a mobster and she loved him with all her heart. That she was marrying Steve because it seemed the right thing to do. Only Lawanna knew the truth.

She had finally told her parents about her gambling problem, the trip to DePaul and the fact that she was an active member of Gamblers Anonymous. But she just hadn't been able to tell them that her upcom-ing marriage would be a sham. It would break their hearts. T.J. was try-ing to decide if she should share her dilemma with her favorite Aunt when Diana walked in.

"What's going on in here?" Diana whispered.

"Nothing, Mama. I'd better get back to the party."

"Me too." Frances followed T.J. out of the library.

"We need to talk some more."

"Thanks, Aunt Fran, but I'll be OK. I'm just getting cold feet. I'll be fine once the whole thing's over with."

*   *   *

A couple of days after T.J.'s lingerie shower, Michael met with Mark O'Keefe. The entire Naughty Games task force team was there at the Rigolets office.

They had been arguing for a couple of hours about how far they could go in their pursuit of Steve Rose and the Louisiana Mob. Especially since John Conti had been ruled out as the head of the organization.

Although they were sure Rose was their man, how to get enough evidence to put him away was causing the dissension among them. And Michael wanted him put away.

"I don't see why we can't pick him up now," Michael insisted. He was willing to do anything to stop T.J. from marrying Rose on Saturday. "We know for sure he's connected to the Mafia."

"Yeah, but although we can make the connection between Rose and the Mob, we can't tie him in to gaming in the State," O'Keefe countered. "You know that. There's no way we can get around the law. We don't know who they're using as a front to provide those slots to the casinos, but you better believe it's a legitimate business."

"OK, how about we get him for bribing the boys in Baton Rouge." Michael suggested.

"You got proof he paid off legislators to turn their heads?"

"I bet he paid them to vote for legalized gambling in Louisiana."

"Bets ain't good enough, Zello."

"How about bugging the place down the road?"

"You know we can't just go in and bug a place on a whim. But, if we could, and I'm not saying we did, we'd know the place hadn't been used since you followed Rose there."

"Well, what can we do?"

The other members of the task force became quiet. They knew this was not just about the Louisiana Mob and gaming in the State. They were aware of Michael's incarceration and figured he had a vendetta going with Rose. They decided to let O'Keefe handle it.

"I tell you what. How about if we get a few good men to flash their badges at Rose's wedding Saturday? No arrests, mind you." Michael's supervisor suggested the plan with a wink.

"I want to be there."

"You'd have to break your cover."

"I've already shown him my hand. It's time to call his. In other words, let it leak that we're planning something Saturday. Don't say what. I want him worried. Very worried."

*   *   *

At 2 a.m. on the day of his wedding, Steve drove to the hide-a-way on Rigolets. He was uncharacteristically a little tipsy.

He had just come from his bachelor party at Inkys, a new seafood place on the levee in Morgan City. T.J.'s father, Tony had hosted the affair and twelve or so of his closest male friends attended. The tables were loaded with bright red crawfish and boiled crabs, corn-on-the-cob, and new potatoes. They were served large frosty pitchers of Dixie beer and some home brew that Inky's son made in his cellar with a kit of some kind.

Steve wasn't sure just how he made the drive from Morgan City to New Orleans and across the Lake, but he had. The call from Frankie made it clear his presence was required.

As he pulled into the parking lot of the deserted restaurant, he noticed Frankie's limo was parked next to the other cars with two of his bodyguards flanking it. Steve sobered up fast. Nothing brought his Godfather this far away from his refuge these days.

A few moments later he was trying to stay calm as he faced Frankie and the group of elderly wiseguys.

"What do you mean, you think they're going to arrest me at my own wedding, for Gods sake?"

"No need to get excited." Joey Romano who had apparently fallen asleep with his eyes opened jerked awake at the sound of the young Don's angry voice. He couldn't believe he'd dropped off in the rare presence of Don Colarossi, but what the hell, it was way past all of their bedtimes. Anyway, he'd opened his mouth, so he might as well continue.

"Not yet, anyway. We don't know how much they overheard."

"Overheard. Overheard? What are you talking about?"

"We found a bug. Under the table," Frank Modella looked under the tablecloth, even though he had removed the device an hour or so earlier. Everyone looked under the table to show they were on the top of things."

"We've been meeting in this place for months and no one thought to check to see if it's been bugged?" Steve asked incredulously.

Frankie Colarossi, who hadn't said much after greeting his Godson with a hug and a peck on both cheeks when he had first entered the room, spoke now.

"We don't know what they know. But word's out you can expect to see the Feds at the church this afternoon. You need to call the wedding off."

"I can't do that."

"Look, Stephano," Frankie said quietly, "They may not know Pietro & Sons, Inc. is connected to us in anyway. I mean the company's been around for thirty years. Strictly legitimate. But, those bastards have something on you. You need to call off the wedding."

"Listen, Godfather. I mean no disrespect. I have to marry T.J. today."

"Why? When you know what could happen."

"Because I love her."

Frankie shrugged his shoulder. "I did'n know."

Joey who had been very upset because he hadn't been invited to the Boss's wedding was sure there was gonna be big trouble at the affair. He mumbled under his breath. "Forget about it. I didn't really want to go in the first place." Then he laid his head back down on the table to take a little nap.

The others kissed the two Dons, then filed out one by one. Steve and Frankie decided it might be dangerous to arouse Joey who'd once dreamed he was taking out a contract and pulled a gun from under his pillow and shot at his cleaning lady. She managed to drop to the floor when she saw the gun, but he never could convince her that he meant her no harm and despite twenty years of service, she'd left. "It's hard to keep good help," was all he ever said about the matter.

As Steve walked Frankie to his limousine, the older man said again, "I really hope you think about my advice and call the whole thing off. I know...you love the girl. But just promise me you'll think about what could happen. **Comprende?**"

"I understand. It's not just T.J. I'm a doctor. A damn good one. People depend on me."

"A lot of good you're going to do them from the slamma."

"Look, I have to get back. I need a few hours sleep. I'll see you at the wedding," Steve said hugging Frankie again.

After Frankie's long black car pulled out, Steve got in his Jag and headed toward Tallula. He needed to do some thinking and the two-hour drive would give him time. He popped his Kenny Rogers' CD in so he could hear the song about the gambler.

Steve had started listening to country-western music when he was in pre-med. His roommate, Danny, was from Nashville and Steve couldn't avoid hearing Garth and George Strait, Reba, Vince and all the rest played night and day in their tiny room. He found country music to be down to earth and although sometimes tragic, often healing. It appealed to his own moody nature that constantly sought equilibrium and peace in his schizophrenic lifestyle. Kenny sang on: You got to know when to hold em, know when to fold em, know when to walk away, know when to run..." Suddenly, Steve made a decision.

Chapter 22

Wedding March???

Miss Emmie looked around the small church. It was only one o'clock and the wedding wasn't scheduled to start until around 2 p.m., but she had arrived early to get a good aisle seat.

The church was much too small to accommodate the hundreds of people expected for the ceremony. They would be standing body to body against the fragile stained-glassed windows that ringed the pews. Just like midnight mass at Easter when the once-a-year Catholics decided to make their Easter duty.

Father Hebert would cringe when he saw those of them who usually made the rounds of bars before they were able to come to confession. Not that a lot of the parishioners still came to confession these days. Anyway, the drunk ones were not especially careful about how they used the beautiful, antique windows for support.

It was very early and the florist was still arranging two huge bouquets of white roses and bridal wreath on the altar. Only a few of the guests had arrived.

Miss Emmie was thankful most people in town had filed their taxes early. Since April 15 fell on a Saturday this year, the few townspeople who held out and refused to take part in the tax revolt would have 'til Monday to file. So Miss Emmie could concentrate on the wedding of the year in Tallula. Actually, this was going to be the town's wedding of all time.

Around 1:30, people started pouring in. Everyone was in a festive mood. The women wore their new Easter pastels for the second time. Since it was still a little cool and most of the outfits were better suited to spring, the ladies wore sweaters or light jackets over their dresses.

Miss Emmie said hello to the Washingtons and Tom and Emelda Walters who walked in together and were escorted to the right of the church, traditionally the groom's side. Today, however, since most of the guests were friends of both T.J. and Steve, the folks could sit anywhere they wanted.

Emmie snickered at Emelda's attire. Overdressed as usual, today she was wearing a man's tux with a very short skirt and a polka-dotted bow tie. She looked like a circus clown in a fat suit, especially since she had overdone the blush. She had painted two perfectly round, bright red spots the size of silver dollars on her lower cheeks.

Julius Green and the La Deauxs were being escorted by a teenage usher whom Miss Emmie had never seen before. She watched as Doc Romero stopped to chat with John Conti and a short, stocky man dressed all in black, grinning from ear to ear. Viola Perkins made it a point to sit directly behind Tom and Emelda Walters, close enough to touch Tom without Emelda noticing if the ceremony moved her to do so.

The Sisters came in together dressed like they were all the mother of the bride. A little too much silk and sequins for the middle of the afternoon, Miss Emmie thought, glancing down at her own tasteful floral cotton dress. She'd bought it at the mall in Houma on sale for $29.99 at Dillards. The Sisters were escorted to the front of the church and were seated on the left in the second pew.

Annie had Carlo in tow—clean and sober for a change. Lucie and James sat arm in arm next to them on the outer aisle in case Lucie had a panic attack and needed to make a fast exit. Frances and Tim

Boudreaux were on the other side of them, dressed in identical Elvis-style jumpsuits. Frances wore all her rings for the occasion.

At about ten minutes before the ceremony was scheduled to begin, Frankie Colarossi and several men dressed in somber dark suits were escorted to a pew in the back of the church. At about the same time, Robert, Tony's brother started to sing. A love song, rather a song about love that Miss Emmie had often heard at mass, but didn't know the name of. Olga Guidry was accompanying him on the organ.

Miss Emmie nodded to a few late arrivals, and waved to Lou Ella Turner and Gaston Long who were standing against the wall, straining to get a view of the altar. Lou Ella wore a bright green sports coat with a orange Saints football team tie.

Robert was singing another song, this time an old favorite of T.J.'s from the Jesus Christ Superstar album she had heard her mother play over and over when she was a child. The song, "I Don't Know How to Love Him" had seemed appropriate for her marriage to Steve whom she had always loved as her best friend.

Cora was being ushered to the front pew with baby Angie in her arms. Both were dressed all in white. Cora wore a big floppy hat with tiny hearts on it and Angie sported a matching headband with one big heart on the side.

After Cora and the baby were seated, Claire Rose was led to the front pew on the left. She wore a hunter green satin dress with straight lines adorned only by a gold necklace that her husband had given her when she was just a bride.

After Claire was settled, Diana was escorted and seated next to Cora. She was dressed in layers, in case one of her dreaded hot flashes brought on by the excitement hit her. She looked quite beautiful in her ivory shantung silk sleeveless dress with a long-sleeve jacket trimmed in gold. She had been crying already, and when she took Angie from Cora's arms, she started again.

It was almost 2 p.m. and the groomsmen were lining up on the altar. Everyone got real quiet in anticipation of the bridesmaids' entrance. All heads turned toward the back of the church.

       *   *   *

T.J. sat alone in the small vestry where Father Hebert and his altar boys and girls usually prepared for mass. The vestry that just moments earlier had been crammed with T.J.'s bridal attendants now had its door closed giving T.J. the few moments of solitude she so desperately needed. She still wasn't sure she was doing the right thing, but she had given her word to Steve and she would keep it.

Tony stuck his head in the door, saw T.J. with her head bowed and decided to let her have her few moments to talk to the Lord. The bridesmaids were lined up, waiting for Steve to join his groomsmen at the altar, so there was time.

Tony gave the bridal coordinator the thumbs up. Suddenly, his stomach started churning and he raced next door to the rectory to use the bathroom there.

Meanwhile in the church, there was one brief moment when everything appeared normal—before all hell broke loose. The guests were getting a little impatient waiting for Steve to join his groomsmen in front of the altar. Olga had just started playing the organ again in anticipation of the bridal party's march down the aisle.

Suddenly, the people were shocked to see about a dozen men wearing blue FBI jackets marching down the aisle instead of the expected bridesmaids. Almost in step to the music, the men moved slowly down the center aisle and planted themselves in a semi-circle around the altar. Father Hebert who had had his last cigarette over thirty minutes earlier, reached under his cassock for one, then realizing where he was, made the sign of the cross instead.

"Oh Lord, help us," Cora shouted, startling Angie who began to wail. "I told those fools not to send that letter to the government." She rocked Angie to quiet her. "Hush, little baby." Then she shouted to the FBI agents.

"They wouldn't listen to me, but I told them it was the devil's doings."

The agents ignored her, but it didn't take long for the dignified moment of anticipation experienced by the wedding guests to change to one of alarm and almost complete pandemonium. They turned to each other in total disbelief that the IRS would be so concerned about their tax protest that they would actually send the Feds to arrest them.

Tom Walters approached one of the agents and started explaining the action.

"I'm an attorney," he whined, "and we have done nothing illegal."

The agent ignored him also and stared straight ahead like one of the guards at Buckingham Palace. In fact, all of the agents seemed to be focusing on the tops of the heads of the townspeople. Not one flicked a muscle, not even when several of the guests started heading for the exits.

In her rush to escape, Emelda shoved Viola Perkins out of the way with such force that the librarian was sure the wife of her lover knew of the affair after all. Tom caught her and sat her down in an empty pew before hurrying after his wife.

Then one of the men in the FBI jackets flashed a badge and addressed the townspeople.

"I want you all to remain calm," he said to loud protests of innocence and a few pleas for mercy. "I just need to know where T.J. is."

The whole church-load of people turned and pointed to the vestry. Michael Zello winked at his baby daughter who had stopped crying and was smiling now, then he headed for the back of the church.

It was at that moment that Cora recognized Michael as Angelo and told Diana who also remembered him from that day he almost drowned in the River behind her house. Diana shared the information with her sisters sitting behind her. Word spread from pew to pew. And what started with "The FBI agent is a friend of the bride" ended being "the FBI agent is a fiend, come for your hide" by the time the message reached Frankie Colarossi and his cronies seated in the back.

The old Don knew why the Feds were here. He laughed as he and his men stepped quietly out of the church, pretending he hadn't seen his grandson with the Addolina idiot. No one made a move to stop them.

After a while, the panic in the room began to die down and the people sat expectantly in their pews. They were torn between rushing home to safety and hanging around to see what would happen next.

                    *   *   *

T.J. was about to step out to tell her dad she was ready when Angelo walked in. She took in his FBI jacket and thought it was just another of his disguises.

"Oh, Angelo, how could you? On my wedding day."

Michael answered by taking T.J. in his arms and kissing her with so much pent-up passion and hunger, all she could do was respond.

"God, I love you, Angelo. On my wedding day. I love you. Oh. My precious Angelo."

"Michael."

"Huh?"

"Your precious Michael. My name is Michael Zello."

Michael took a few moments to tell T.J. everything. Including the part about Steve Rose being the head of the Louisiana Mob.

"Steve? Did you arrest Steve? Did you arrest my groom? My God, Angelo, I mean Michael. You have the wrong man. Don't you think I'd know if my best friend whom I've known and loved since we were kids was in the Mafia?"

"Calm down, darling. We haven't arrested him. He's not even here."

"What do you mean, he's not here? We're getting married in a few moments. He'd better be here. I'll kill him if he left me standing at the altar."

"T.J., you've got to get a hold of yourself. You don't really want to marry him. You want to marry me. Don't you?"

"Yes, I want to marry you, but...are you really an FBI agent? Not in the Mob? Not a loan shark? But you loaned me the money?"

"All part of my job. Look, I'll tell you about it later. Meanwhile there's a whole bunch of folks out there waiting for a wedding. We don't want to disappoint them, do we?"

Michael walked to the front of the church, whispered something to Father Hebert, who had ducked behind the ornate altar to have a couple of cigarettes while all the humbug was going on. Meanwhile, T.J. found Tony who had just returned from the bathroom and had missed out on all the excitement. She asked him to bring Diana to the vestry for a quick chat. A little while later T.J. and Lawanna huddled together for a few moments and the rest of the bridesmaids were informed of a slight change of plans.

The only bridesmaid who thought T.J. might be nuts was her cousin, Jessie. Jessie and T.J. were only a few months apart but didn't know each other very well. She had grown up in San Antonio and because her daddy, Uncle Pete, rarely returned to Tallula, the girls were practically strangers. Mama had insisted T.J. have her as a bridesmaid, because that's how Italian families did things. So when Jessie gave T.J. a look that said, "What am I doing in this zoo?" T.J. just hugged her cousin and said, "Welcome to the real world." Both girls laughed.

*   *   *

Father Hebert stood up and said he had to make an announcement.

"The wedding between T.J. and Stephen is being called off. I don't know exactly why, but it might have something to do with the fact that Steve didn't show up. I don't know exactly why he left T.J. standing at the altar, but I'm sure we'll find out soon enough."

The priest waited for the surprised guests to absorb that bit of information before continuing. They had received enough shock for one day. Even though the FBI agents had moved and were now lined up where Steve's groomsmen had stood before.

"Now, I have another announcement." Father Hebert decided it was safe to continue, since no one had passed out from the hullabaloo so far.

"Teresa Jude Marino and Mr. Michael Zello who is with the Federal Bureau of Investigation will be getting married instead and you're all invited." He ranted on about pre-cana conference and marriage licenses and blood work and numerous other reasons the wedding wouldn't be strictly legal.

"So even though we might have to do it all over again to make it take, in the eyes of the good Lord and the law, these two young people will be man and wife. Now if we're ready to begin."

Everyone applauded their approval, then once again turned to the back of the church as Olga started playing the organ.

Epilogue
Wedding March

As the lovely bridesmaids wearing short teal-blue dresses started down the aisle, Lawanna whispered to her friend.

"What am I gonna do without you, Girl. I'm gonna be bored to death without all the nonsense that goes on in your life."

"I just realized, I'm marrying Angelo. I mean Michael. I don't even know where I'm going to be living. Maybe we'll be in New Orleans. Wouldn't that be wonderful? You'd still be around to take care of me when my life gets too crazy."

T.J. realized that everyone was staring at her and her best friend who should be halfway down the aisle by now.

"Go," she said. "Wait." T.J. grabbed her dear friend and hugged her tightly. "Now go."

She watched Lawanna march slowly down the aisle, noticing her friend had lost several pounds and must have given up chocolate in preparation for the wedding. Her dress was a little darker and longer than those of the other attendants. She looked wonderful.

Before T.J. knew it, it was her turn. Her daddy looked a little pale, but he was used to being in the limelight and T.J. knew he would be OK.

Tony took his daughter's arm and started to escort her slowly toward the altar as Olga played "Here Comes the Bride" to the tears and smiles

of most everyone in the church. As they approached the altar, Tony
pulled T.J. closer and squeezed her arm.

Miss Emmie paid little attention to the ceremony. She had attended
lots of Catholic weddings over the years and they were always the same
as far as she was concerned. She was much more interested in the reaction of her friends and neighbors.

They seemed to have forgotten the earlier threat of arrest and were
held enraptured by the young couple exchanging vows. Father Hebert
had to improvise and several times during the ceremony referred to the
groom as Stephen instead of Michael which didn't bother T.J. too much
since she still thought of the man she was marrying as Angelo.

As Miss Emmie scanned the faces in the church, she thought of how
fond she was of most of the wedding guests. She realized that even if the
FBI had come for them instead of T.J., they would have handled it
together as they had handled so many moments of crisis in Tallula over the
years. Hurricane Andrew being the most memorable one when they had to
band together to help each other put their homes and lives back together.

Miss Emmie observed The Sisters as each, with tears in her eyes,
watched proudly as T.J. married the man she loved. Everything was for-
given at weddings. The Sisters, despite their different personalities and
physical appearances and sometimes fiery disagreements, were totally
devoted to each other. In a show of support and love, each placed a
hand on Diana's shoulders who was sobbing with joy as she marveled
at and thanked God for her daughter's happiness.

Diana kissed Tony on the cheek and raised Angie on her shoulder so
she could watch her mama and daddy get married. T.J. had decided not to
have a wedding mass because it would make the ceremony too long and
she was concerned about all her menopausal relatives. So before she knew
it, Father Hebert was pronouncing her and Michael "man and wife."

Angelo, she told herself. You married Angelo. She didn't have too
much time to absorb all that happened. For one fleeting moment, she
wondered where Steve was, hoping he was safe and out of the FBI's

reach, but then Michael was kissing her and everyone was applauding Mr. and Mrs. Michael Zello.

Someone, probably Lana Rosenberg, shouted "Mazel Tov" and then John Conti's companion picking up the cry, shouted, "Molotov" and the FBI agents all drew their weapons thinking someone had a bomb. Some of the guests screamed and held up their hands. After the agents realized there was no real danger, they put away their guns. Then they formed a line on either side of T.J and Michael, ready to escort the bridesmaids down the aisle after the bride and groom made their exit.

T.J. walked over to her parents and kissed each on cheek, saying "thank you." Then she took her baby from her mother, touched Cora gently on the cheek and joined Michael. He took Angie from T.J, kissed them both, then walked his family down the aisle and into the bright sunshine.

They didn't notice the young man watching from the back seat of Frankie Colarossi's old black limo. Steve waited until T.J and Michael entered their own limousine, then with a sad, knowing smile, motioned for the driver to start the car.

"This isn't over, T.J. my darling," Steve whispered as the car moved slowly away from the church and the hometown he loved.

About the Author

L.L. Lee

L.L. Lee's, first book, *How To Survive Menopause Without Going Crazy*, was published in 1998. *Taxing Tallulah* is her first novel. She is currently writing another humorous novel that also involves her native Louisiana. Ms. Lee is a registered nurse with degrees in psychology & English.